DE
HIGHLAND HEAVYWEIGHT

Jayne E. Self

DEATH OF A HIGHLAND HEAVYWEIGHT

Contact Information: titleadmin@pelicanbookgroup.com

Cover Art by Nicola Martinez

Harbourlight Books, a division of Pelican Ventures, LLC
www.pelicanbookgroup.com PO Box 1738 *Aztec, NM * 87410

Publishing History
First Harbourlight Edition, 2012
Print Edition ISBN 978-1-61116-196-0
Electronic Edition ISBN 978-1-61116-195-3
Published in the United States of America

Dedication

God has blessed me greatly.
To the men in my life: my incredible husband Harvey, my three amazing sons, Allan, Jamie, and Jon, and my extraordinaire grandson, Cameron.
Thanks also to Jean, Tracey, Jamie, and Nicola, who helped make this story happen.

Praise for Jayne E. Self

Murder in Hum Harbour

Jayne E. Self provides us with a fresh voice in mystery fiction. *Murder in Hum Harbour* is a fast-paced mystery filled with characters that might force one to look askance at one's own neighbors. ~ Janet Benrey, author Pippa Hunnechurch Mysteries

I read *Murder in Hum Harbour* with delight. The lively cast of characters brings this small Nova Scotia town fully to life. The main character—whose faith is tinged with humour and grounded in trust—was completely engaging. Twists and turns carry the reader along to the final surprising climax. The romantic subplots add zest. A job well done. ~ Rosemary Aubert, author of the Ellis Portal Mystery Series

I immediately fell in love with the main character. *Murder in Hum Harbour* is a lovely little cozy mystery which kept me guessing throughout. Jayne Self is an author to watch! ~ Linda Hall author of *Steal Away* and *Sadie's Song*

1

It started with the robberies. I doubt anyone would have noticed anything missing if Mom and I hadn't been browsing through wedding magazines at my place. We were searching for the perfect bridesmaid dress, one that would suit both my sister-in-law, Sasha, and my cousin, Ashleigh, when Mom mentioned she couldn't find her kitchen frog—you know, those little ceramic creatures that hold pot scrubby pads.

Ash is a frog fanatic. She collects frog everything, which was why frogs and bridesmaid dresses went together in Mom's mind.

"Come to think of it," I said, leaning back to see into my postage stamp kitchen, "I haven't seen mine for a while either."

I live above my shop, Dunmaglass, and after last year's break-in, I'd installed a mega security system. No one should be able to sneak in and abscond with anything—even my kitchen frog.

"We should report the thefts to the police. Andrew's been complaining that business is dull this summer."

My brother, Andrew, was one of three local law enforcement officers.

Mom closed the magazine and reached for a new one. "Don't go wishing for another crime spree, Gailynn MacDonald. We've had enough in this town to last a lifetime."

"I don't think the Simmons brothers getting caught siphoning gas for their lawnmower constitutes a crime spree, Mom."

"Neither is a couple of missing kitchen frogs."

"You never know," I said. "First kitchen frogs, then small appliances, freezers. Imagine the hoopla if we had a ring of freezer raiders on our hands."

I clicked my tongue as Mom wiped laughter-tears from her cheeks.

"You laugh now, but mark my words, this is bigger than a couple of kitchen frogs."

She pushed her new magazine across the table. "Look, I've found the perfect dress."

I was doubtful, but Mom, an avid sewer, sees things I miss at first glance.

She tapped the picture with her finger. "All we need to do is change the shoulders, tuck the waist a bit, and lengthen the hem. We could even eliminate the lace ruffles, if you like." She smiled triumphantly.

"And it'll have to be lavender."

"Purple?" She crinkled her nose with disdain.

"Lavender. Otherwise it's perfect."

And that was the last time I thought about missing kitchen frogs until I discovered Carrie Hunter-Oui administering CPR to her husband in the middle of her back hallway.

2

I was trekking home along the widening band of gravel seashore, silently lamenting the depressingly few pieces of sea glass I'd collected during my morning walk. What with plastic bottles and recycling, there were fewer and fewer bits of colored glass washing up on the beach. I suppose I could have seen the famine as the proverbial silver lining; less sea glass meant my jewelry would become rare, which meant I could hike prices. But I didn't find it encouraging. I liked making jewelry, and Dunmaglass—the exclusive distributor of my authentic sea glass jewelry—was doing very well that summer. I'd even hired Ashleigh to staff the shop while I was busy at the medical clinic.

I swung my arms as I marched, enjoying the way the sun electrified my diamond ring, and shunted sparks of rainbow light onto the wet rocks. It was going to be a warm day. Already the air felt thick enough to slice.

I'd reached the edge of town. Hunter Hall, Hum Harbour's oldest building, a rambling two-storey structure made of Scottish rock, towered above. The original owner imported the quarried stones direct from the holy land itself. These days, the place was part business and part house. Carrie Hunter-Oui, owner/manager of Hunter Monuments and Toys, lived on the premises with her famous husband, Claude Oui.

Claude—Wee Claude to his fans—was our

National Highland Heavyweight Champion. He could toss a caber further than anyone in the world and looked magnificent doing it.

From where I stood, I could see the last of the fishing fleet chugging past the giant rocks that mark Hum Harbour's entrance, and it reminded me that if I didn't get a leg on, I'd be late opening the clinic where I was medical receptionist. I'm pretty sure that's when the screaming started.

Shrill, hair-splitting shrieks, mixed with the unmistakable howls of a basset hound, erupted from Hunter Hall. I vaulted the stone retaining wall, jumped over the compost pile, and raced up the sloping lawn to the house. I've never taken Carrie for a screamer, she's too tall, so I knew whatever was wrong was dead serious.

I shoved open the French door, and almost tripped over the hound in my hurry to reach Carrie.

She was kneeling at the base of the stairs. Elbows turned outward, she leaned heavily on her hands, as she performed CPR on Claude. With each thrust, the gemstone she always wore around her neck flashed as it caught a beam of sunlight, as if blinking a warning. Between chest compressions, she threw back her head and hollered at the top of her lungs. Caber, the hound, howled in unison.

I could tell in an instant Carrie's technique wouldn't save her husband. Sadly, nothing would. The dark staining of his skin told me he'd been gone for a while. I grabbed the phone and dialed 911.

3

I managed to pry Carrie from her husband's side and drag her into the kitchen.

In the two or three minutes it took Andrew to arrive, sirens blaring, I plugged in the tea kettle. When Andrew's car screeched to a halt in front of the house, I let my brother in.

"You?" he shouted over Caber's mournful howl. Evidently, the dispatcher hadn't alerted Andrew that I was the one who called.

I led him to the base of the back stairs. Claude Oui was a Goliath of a man. Six-five, two hundred eighty-five pounds. Stretched out on the floor like he was, Claude took up most of the hallway, and apart from being dead, he looked pretty much like he always did. A kind, gentle-faced giant.

"What happened?" asked Andrew.

"I'm not sure. I heard Carrie's screams, and when I ran in, I found her doing CPR on Claude."

Andrew crouched beside the body. "Ambulance is on its way, though I guess there's no need to hurry."

I wrapped my arms around my waist, warding off a sudden chill. "I'm not sure how much Carrie'll be able to tell you. I think she's in shock."

"You think?" Andrew pushed to his feet.

"Can I cover him with a blanket?"

"Need to check the scene first." He squared his shoulders. "And talk to Carrie."

"She's in the kitchen."

Andrew had left the front door open, and Geoff—my incredibly handsome fiancé who also happens to be Hum Harbour's only doctor—wandered in. He wore his jogging duds.

"I heard the sirens, saw Andrew's car. What's wrong, Gai?"

I closed and latched the door behind him. We didn't need a crowd. "It's Claude."

"What? I just saw him last night." Geoff hurried deeper into the house and found Claude, and howling Caber, in the hall. "Dear Lord," he whispered and made the sign of the cross. It was something he'd picked up during his five years as a missionary in Africa. People found habits like that comforting, and everyone knows those poor people in Somalia needed all the comfort they could get.

Kneeling, Geoff gently closed Claude's eyes. "This is my fault. I should have taken last night more seriously."

"What do you mean?"

"I met Claude while he was out walking Caber, and he invited me back to the house to talk. I was still here when Danny-Boy Murdock stopped by."

Andrew reappeared. "Murdock was here?"

"Came banging on the door around nine-thirty."

Andrew scribbled in his notepad. "Know what he wanted?"

Geoff brushed his hand across his eyes. The gesture mimicked the way he'd touched Claude, as though closing his own eyes to the terrible scene before him. "He was upset about the Highland Ale endorsement. Murdock never thought much of Claude's conversion or his plans to go to Ghana, but he was eager to cash in on it. He'd expected Claude to endorse him as Highland Ale's new spokesman when he withdrew from the contract. So they argued."

"Punches exchanged?"

"Murdock knocked Claude down."

I gasped. "He what?"

Danny-Boy Murdock was also a highland heavyweight competitor, but he wasn't the athlete Claude was. It surprised me he could get the draw on Claude.

"It seemed harmless enough, at the time. I told Murdock to get lost before I called the police, then I checked Claude, as much as he'd let me. I thought he was fine." Geoff's worried frown deepened the clefts in his cheeks. "How could I have missed this?"

Pen poised in the air, Andrew focused on Geoff. "You think Claude's death was Murdock's fault?"

"I don't know. But with Claude's medical history, I should have been more insistent. I knew the punch and the fall could have serious consequences. But he promised to tell Carrie what happened as soon as she got home from her meeting, and she knew what symptoms to watch for. She'd take him to Antigonish at the first sign of trouble." Antigonish, a college town about a half hour away, had the closest hospital.

Not everyone knew that Claude suffered from PCS. Post Concussion Syndrome. It plagued a lot of big-name athletes, hockey players, football stars, boxers. Over the years Claude had endured his share of head injuries, but the most serious happened a year earlier when Danny-Boy beaned Claude during a hammer toss.

I don't imagine anyone could forget the incident. The bleachers were full, and more fans were cheering from their lawn chairs or on blankets on the grass. Danny-Boy swung the hammer in an arc above his head, when suddenly the 22-pound ball broke from the handle and hurtled toward the other competitors. Wee Claude saw it coming and shoved two men out of the way. He got hit.

The shocked silence of the watching crowd still rang in my ears.

Everyone thought Claude was finished, and no one had the heart to go on without him, so they cancelled the rest of the competition. Miraculously, Claude rallied. He was out of the hospital within the week and went on to win that year's International Highland Heavyweight Championship.

Now Claude was dead, and Danny-Boy, once again, was involved. Maybe.

Andrew snapped his little book closed and popped it into his breast pocket. "Well, looks like Carrie must have missed something."

4

Andrew trotted back to the kitchen, and I followed, leaving Geoff and Claude alone. My brother's not the most tactful man in the world, and I didn't want him upsetting Carrie unnecessarily. Not on top of everything else.

He pulled out a chair and straddled it, his arms crossed along its ladder-back. "Carrie, can I ask you a couple of questions?"

She sat with her elbows on the kitchen's trestle table, her head in her hands. She looked up slowly. Scrubbing her palm across her face, she wiped away most of her tears.

"Carrie, tell Andrew what happened," I said in what I hoped was an encouraging tone.

"I came downstairs this morning and…and…there was Claude on the floor at the bottom of the stairs. I…he…oh, mercy." She sucked in a quivering breath. "I wasn't sure what to do. I've never taken CPR. I should have, I know I should have, but Claude's so vital and strong, I just never imagined…"

Rudely, the kettle's whistle blared. I ripped the plug from the socket.

Andrew flashed me an annoyed look as the silence echoed through the stone-walled kitchen. Maybe, like me, the sudden stillness reminded him of the last time Claude was hurt. "Did Claude tell you Murdock knocked him down last night?"

Carrie's eyes widened. "What? No. That man was here, in my house?"

Andrew inclined his head, yes. "So Claude didn't tell you to keep an eye out for any of his concussion symptoms?"

"I always keep an eye on Claude, ever since his diagnosis. Geoff says Claude's condition makes him fragile. He can't afford another head injury, so I've been especially watchful. It drives Claude crazy." Her face crumpled. "It drove ..."

"So he was fine when you went to bed last night."

"Yes. I went ahead upstairs, and he turned out the lights."

"What time?"

"I don't know. Eleven-thirty?"

"Claude joined you?"

Her cheeks flushed. "I fell asleep so fast. I was exhausted after the meeting last night. I'm really not sure." Last night's meeting of the Hum Harbour Daze festival Steering Committee, of which I am also a member, had dragged on until practically eleven.

Andrew turned to me. "You were at the same meeting, Gai. You can confirm Carrie was there?"

"Of course," I said, surprised. "It was our second last meeting. Lasted from seven 'til after ten-thirty. I still had a headache when I got up this morning."

Andrew nodded. "OK, you got home before eleven. You went to bed. Hear anything unusual during the night?"

"I slept straight through until six-thirty this morning. That's when I found Claude. I thought maybe he'd slipped on his way downstairs or something, so I tried doing CPR the best I could but..."

"You were doing fine," I said. "It was just too

late."

Andrew's eyes darkened sympathetically. "What time did Claude normally get up?"

"Five, when he was training." A hint of a smile crossed her lips. "He was always training. He loved the games so much."

The warble of the approaching ambulance's siren drowned out whatever Andrew said next. "…will have to be checked by the medical examiner." Andrew returned his chair to its place against the wall. "Gai, can you stay with her?"

"Of course."

"Afterwards, Carrie, if you could have a look around the house, tell me if anything's out of place."

"Why?" I asked.

"Just need to make sure we don't miss anything."

Carrie dropped her chin into her hands. "Sure, whatever."

I went back to making tea.

There was a fair bit of commotion as the emergency personnel removed Claude. I stayed with Carrie, like Andrew asked, and fed her tea and toast. She didn't eat more than a bite, but the fussing gave me something to do. Carrie and I weren't particularly close, and I didn't want to impose on her grief. I didn't want her to start screaming again, either, so I maintained a quiet presence, hoping it would be more conducive to calm than an overly sympathetic one.

The grandfather clock beside the dish dresser slowly ticked off the minutes.

In time, Andrew reappeared in the kitchen doorway and asked Carrie to join him. "I know this is hard," he said. "But if you could stroll through the house and the shop, see if there's anything disturbed or missing."

"You think Claude caught a burglar in the act?"

"Anything's possible," he said. "Just want you to tell me what you see."

I followed Carrie and Andrew on their tour through the old house. I was curious. Hunter Hall always reminded me of a mausoleum. Probably because of the tombstones arrayed in the front parlor, the showroom of Hunter Monuments. As I surveyed the house, however, with its dark paneled walls, heavy brocade drapes, and blackened Jacobean antiques, I gained a new appreciation for the word creepy. Carrie's whimsical folk art collection did nothing to lighten the ambiance. In fact, I thought it made it worse.

The back hallway seemed enormous without Claude, and the carpeted stairs were so steep I could barely make out the top.

"What do you see?" Andrew asked Carrie. "Anything unusual?"

She squeezed her face between her hands and looked around. "The carpet?"

"What about the carpet?"

"That step near the top. The runner looks loose."

I saw nothing significant, but Andrew climbed the stairs to check. Second from the top he stooped and picked up a slim, brass rod. "Hmm."

"What is it?" Carrie asked.

"Carpet rod's just lying here. Runner's not clamped down."

Now that Claude had been transferred to the ambulance and taken away, Geoff reappeared. He draped his arm over my shoulders, and I leaned into him, hoping his body heat would stop my shivers.

"You think Claude slipped on the loose rug?"

"We'll wait and see what the medical examiner says." Andrew carried the slim brass rod down the stairs. "In the meantime, Carrie, I'll have an officer come by and take some pictures. OK? What else?"

She glanced around. "Nothing really."

Geoff said, "That candlestick on the hall table was at the top of the stairs when I was here last night."

I studied the item in question, part of Carrie's folk-art collection. It looked kind of like a totem pole made up completely of frogs, and it stood almost half a meter high. What was it with people and their frogs?

Carrie picked up the candlestick, a smile almost lifting the corners of her mouth. "Claude always says you stop seeing things around you when they're always the same. So we play this game where he's forever moving my frogs." She set it down, her fingers lingering over the candlestick's colorful surface. "He's right, you know. I usually keep the pair on the table at the top of the stairs."

"They were up top when I used the bathroom last night," said Geoff. "Where's the second one?"

Carrie spun in a slow circle. "It has to be here somewhere. I just have to look until I find it."

Andrew examined the one candlestick without touching it. "We'll bag this, check it for prints."

She did the face squeeze thing again. "I'm sure mine and Claude's will be all over it."

Andrew waved away her concern with a flip of his notepad. "I'm interested in other prints. We'll take yours for elimination purposes, though."

"Do you see anything else out of place?" I asked.

She wandered into her living room/great room. One entire end of the room was fireplace. You could have held a dance in it. There were twin horsehair sofas, four winged-back chairs, a pair of squat, black side-tables, and a museum's worth of folk art frogs. Frogs on the tables. Frogs on the mantle. Frogs on the walls. They came in every color, size, and style. If only Ash could have seen them.

Carrie scanned the room, and I heard her counting under her breath. I guessed she was counting frogs. She reached one hundred and seven and stopped. Her lips pursed, she started again while we watched in fascination.

The second time Carrie reached a hundred and seven, she grabbed Andrew's arm for support. "I've been robbed!" She started shrieking all over again.

5

"I bet it's the frog thief," I said. "Even her kitchen frog is missing."

We were back in Carrie Hunter's picture-perfect kitchen. Despite the summer heat outside, I found Hunter Hall chilly. Andrew and I huddled around the kitchen table, sipping tea from frog-faced mugs, while a second police officer inspected the house, snapping photos. A box of bagged whatevers sat on the counter, awaiting Andrew's departure.

Geoff stepped into the room.

"How is she?" Andrew asked.

Geoff poured tea from the bullfrog teapot into another froggy mug. "She's in shock, poor thing. I gave her a sedative, and she's fallen asleep. Hopefully, she'll be a little calmer when she wakes up." He pulled up a chair and joined us at the table.

"I wish I knew who to call," I said. "She really shouldn't be left here alone, even if she is asleep."

Geoff studied me over the rim of his mug. "Does that mean you're volunteering?"

How could I not? Carrie was an only child. Her father, Fraser Hunter, had passed way several years before, and her mom, Phyllis, lived in a retirement home. As far as I knew, Carrie had no other relatives in Nova Scotia.

"The clinic schedule's pretty quiet today. I think your boss can manage without you for one day," Geoff said.

"And our appointment with the jeweler about your wedding ring?"

His dimples deepened. "We can rebook." We'd done it before.

"About the frog thief." I turned to Andrew. "You should probably talk to Ash about that."

My brother pushed back his chair. "There's no frog thief, Gai."

"Yes, there is. Mom and I were talking about it just the other day. Someone's been slipping into people's houses and stealing their kitchen frogs."

"Kitchen frogs?" repeated Geoff.

"Those little ceramic things you keep your pot scrubbing pads in."

"Why would anyone take kitchen frogs?"

"I haven't the foggiest. Until I saw Carrie's collection, I though Ash was the only person on earth with a frog fetish. Who knows, maybe frogs are the latest thing in home decor."

Andrew gave me his most dubious stare.

"I'm serious. People collect pigs, cows, roosters. Why not frogs?"

"Has anyone lifted your frog?"

"As a matter of fact."

Geoff set his frog mug next to Andrew's and massaged the bridge of his nose.

"I'm not making this up. And if they're somehow involved in Claude's death, that means they've graduated from petty criminals into felons."

"We don't have felons in Canada, Gai."

"Then what are they?"

"Murderers."

Andrew's pronouncement helped Geoff regain his

composure. "You really think Claude was murdered?"

"If the house was burgled last night, I have to take the possibility seriously. I've notified RCMP's Serious Crime Task Force, and they'll oversee the investigation, on paper at least. I'll do the local leg work."

I felt called upon to point out, "Which you'll enjoy."

"Yeah, but murder's never a good thing, no matter how intriguing the puzzle."

"Where do you go from here?" asked Geoff.

"We've checked the scene, taken our pictures, and bagged any evidence, for what it's worth. Now I establish the time line."

"Don't you already know it? I mean, Carrie told you when she last saw Claude."

Andrew patted the little notebook in his shirt pocket. "And once I confirm her statement, I start investigating suspects."

"You should talk to Ash," I said, again. "She'll know something, I'm sure of it."

Andrew brushed off my advice. "If I need to speak with Ashleigh at some point, I will. But right now I have more important things to do."

An unsettling shiver slid down my spine as, anticipating their departure, I glanced around the expansive kitchen. "You're both going to leave me here, alone?"

"Gai, if you're right, and this is a crime scene, I don't need half of Hum Harbour parading through this house."

"I know, but—"

"I thought Carrie was your friend."

I looked from Geoff to Andrew to Caber, who'd parked himself on my left foot. "I really don't know her that well. I mean, I know we've been working together on the Hum Harbour Daze stuff, but Carrie's well, you know."

Andrew quirked his brow, a talent I've tried desperately to mimic. "No, I don't know."

I tugged at my ponytail. "She's polite and all, but she makes it pretty clear I'm not a Hunter Hall kind of girl, if you know what I mean?"

Geoff's eyes narrowed. "She insults you?"

"No, it's nothing like that. It's just a feeling I get. She's pretty choosy about who she lets beyond the front shop. If she hadn't been in such a panic, I doubt she would have let me in the house even today."

Andrew stood. "Well, she has now, so you may as well make the most of the opportunity. If Carrie Hunter's as exclusive as you think, she'll send you packing the moment she wakes up."

That was probably true. I suspected even in grief Carrie Hunter'd prefer privacy. But I would stay until she insisted I leave, because no one should be alone at a time like this. I just wished Hunter Hall was more inviting. There was something unnerving about a zillion folk art frogs watching your every move.

Geoff understood. "You don't like it here, do you?"

I kissed him. "I'll be OK. Are you sure you won't need me at the clinic?"

"I need you, truly. But for this one day I think I can manage the place without you." He squeezed my hand. "Granted, it won't be the same, nothing is ever the same when you're not there, but I will survive. Somehow."

Such hogwash. I kissed him again.

While we were occupied, Andrew grabbed his box

of evidence and left.

Geoff followed soon after.

I pulled down the blinds in the front rooms, and secured the CLOSED sign on the Hall's front door. News travels at warp speed in Hum Harbour, but I didn't want to chance that someone missed the newsflash and wandered in, searching for marble monuments or German toys.

The front half of the main floor of Hunter Hall houses the Hunter's family business, Hunter Monuments and Toys. For years, it had just been Hunter Monuments but when Carrie came onboard she added the Toy Room. Fortunately, you don't have to pass through the monument showroom to access her inventory of imported toys. Once you step through the Hall's arched double doorway you turn right for toys or left for tombstones.

I locked the door, marched right past both "shops," and mounted the steep back stairs. I'd check Carrie. And maybe, while I was at it, I'd look around the oldest building in Hum Harbour. Andrew was right, of course. This was too good an opportunity to pass up.

6

Carrie was asleep in the room closest to the top of the stairs. I peered in cautiously, not wanting to invade her privacy. But I could hardly keep a watchful eye if I didn't know where she was.

Stretched almost the length of her king-size bed, with her hair fanned across the pillow, she reminded me of a sleeping princess. It didn't seem right for Carrie to look so peaceful. Surely it was Geoff's sedative that relaxed her elegant features and gave her that carefree look.

Ignoring Caber, who was virtually stuck like glue to my heel, I crept into the room, lifted the ivory afghan from a winged chair in the corner—almost knocking over the small, chair-side table in the process—and spread the cover over her. I gave the room a quick survey before I left. Good thing, too, because I spotted Carrie's necklace on the floor beneath the little table. An emerald surrounded by diamonds that trailed away in cuts of decreasing size, kind of like a comet's tail—Carrie's necklace was legendary in these parts.

You see, Carrie Hunter came from a long line of Hunters. The original ones arrived on the HMS Humphrey, the ship that brought the first Scottish settlers to our harbor. That fact means nothing to anyone except the Hunters. But when Carrie met and fell in love with Claude Oui, the oldest of nine kids from a poor Cape Breton family, her parents were less than thrilled. They had standards, after all. And Claude simply didn't measure up. To prove his worthiness, he bought Carrie a stunning emerald and diamond necklace. I guess it was his way of demonstrating how he would provide for their daughter. It must have worked, because the Hunters gave their blessing to the marriage. Claude and Carrie ended up living in the same house with them for years.

The necklace must have fallen from the table when I bumped it. I set it back on top and slipped out of the room before I caused more damage.

With all the doors along the corridor closed, the hallway was cave dark. I felt my way along the passage, checking each room to make sure there was no one else home besides Carrie, Caber, and me.

The first room, I assumed, had been her parents' bedroom, with its giant curtained bed, massive dressers, and carved oak mantle. The next two rooms were guest rooms with bookshelves and antique coverlet-draped beds, and finally, I discovered two home offices.

The first office was Carrie's. No one else could tolerate the gilt-framed frog portrait that dominated the room. It was done in an art-deco style, all golden light and cerulean sky. Might have been nice, except for the frogs in Grecian gowns. The furniture was a hodgepodge of eras; a roll top desk, a fiberboard computer station, and the kind of shelves that rest on metal, wall-mounted brackets. They held an assortment of product catalogues for the various toy lines Carrie sold. There were also monument catalogues, which I curiously flipped through.

The desk phone rang.

I debated whether to answer. What should I say? How would I field the obvious questions from whoever was on the other end? At the third ring the machine kicked in, and I didn't have to decide.

Claude's office/workout room opened off an adjoining door. Exercise equipment filled most of the space. A giant fan filled the window—which might have explained why the room didn't smell like a sweat shop. A heart rate vs. weight chart hung on the wall. There were also framed pictures of Claude in his kilt balancing a caber, chucking a hammer, and several of him accepting trophies. A framed collection of trading cards showed how his body had matured over the years. In the corner sat a leather recliner chair, and a small bookshelf. I recognized some of the dog-eared volumes Geoff'd brought back from Somalia, among the shelf's newer titles. And there was also a journal. I sank into Claude's chair, considering whether to read it. Maybe, between his reflections on his wife and his life, I'd discover a few comments about my Geoff—not that I was prying.

The phone rang again. Like a shout from my conscience, it had me stuffing Claude's journal back onto the shelf between *Mary Slessor of Calabar* and *A Guide to West Africa*. The machine took over after the third ring, and Carrie, bless her heart, slept on.

A bulletin board with a map of Africa rested against Claude's shelf. A big red circle surrounded Ghana.

I've never yearned to travel, even though most people who grow up in small towns can't wait to leave. Like Geoff, who headed for Africa as soon as he graduated medical school, they can't wait to see new places. I traced the red circle with my fingertip and tried to imagine what Ghana would be like.

It wasn't much more than a year since Claude Oui had given his heart to the Lord. He'd caused quite a stir in the local churches. I mean, it wasn't often that an international athlete of Claude's caliber made an open, life-changing profession of faith. Everyone knew. Everyone talked about it. Everyone scrutinized Claude's movements, trying to judge for themselves whether his new-found faith was for real.

Claude's conversion coincided with Geoff's return after five years on a medical mission in Somalia. Claude was fascinated by Geoff's experiences, convicted by the stories of infinite need, and challenged to use his own life to make a difference. I suspect that's why he planned the trip to Ghana.

Claude had been excited when he told Geoff of his decision to trade competitive athletics for the mission field. Carrie, he insisted, would back him one-hundred percent, once she got over the shock. It had been several months since Claude announced his intentions. Presumably, Carrie'd come to terms with his vision.

Not that it mattered now.

Geoff said mission work wasn't for everyone. He said people in Hum Harbour needed God's love every bit as much as people in Africa or Asia. I knew he meant well when he told me that. He didn't want me thinking I was a second-class Christian just because I didn't want to leave Canada.

Deep inside I wondered, though; was I committed to Canada because I cared about my neighbors, or because I was afraid to try something different? Because the very thought of dipping my toes in change terrified me as much as the idea of dipping my toes into the sea. And believe me, after almost drowning twice, I would not—for any reason—dip my toes in the ocean. Ever again.

Speaking of toes, Caber pawed impatiently at mine. I took him out into the backyard where he investigated the lawn for unidentified odors, and I investigated Carrie's garden.

I'm not big on gardening, but I do appreciate well-tended flower beds. Like my mom and my cousin, Mimi—both gardening fanatics—it seemed Carrie rearranged and expanded her plantings regularly. I could see where she'd been digging most recently. I thought she was moving daylilies. Or maybe they were oriental lilies.

The phone rang three times and stopped. Caber and I went back inside. I sat at the kitchen table; he sat on my feet. The clock ticked, and Carrie slept on. To fill the time, and to keep my mind from murder, I read the paper.

7

My cousin, Mimi—owner of the Hubris Heron Seafood Café, and a fabulous cook—saved me from a boring editorial on the FBI's failure to catch some jewel thief working the Atlantic seaboard. According to the paper, the guy'd escaped into Canada. Like we wanted him?

Mimi's an incredible woman. Last year, when Doc Campbell died, I accused her of murder in front of half the town. My cheeks still burn when I remember how badly I behaved. But Mimi forgave me. How amazing is that?

She banged on the kitchen's French door, a blue cooler sitting beside her feet.

I helped her lift it inside.

"I can't believe it," she said after her hug. "How could this happen to someone as strong as Wee Claude?" When she shook her head, her auburn curls bounced furiously. "I brought a few things for Carrie to have on hand when people call." Mimi unloaded a meat tray, veggie tray, fruit tray, biscuits, jellied salad, casserole, pie, and two trays of assorted squares and oat cakes. I tried stacking them in the fridge—not an easy job in Carrie's narrow side-by-side—and a few carrot sticks slid off the veggie tray. I poked them back into place.

"Are you going to be all right?" she asked.

"Me?" I slammed the fridge shut. "This whole

business is tragic—freakishly tragic—and like everyone else I'm shocked. But it's nothing compared to what Carrie must be feeling. We're not close, Carrie and me, you know that." I swallowed hard. "But ever since this morning I've had this burning lump in my throat."

She hunkered down and massaged Caber's droopy ears. "All those years I worked with Carrie on the committee, she never invited me inside Hunter Hall. I thought maybe you and she had discovered more in common."

"Geoff gave her a sedative, and I said I'd keep watch while she sleeps. She needs a friend, someone she doesn't mind crying in front of."

"Good luck with that. Carrie's a loner. Claude, her parents, I don't know anyone else she's close to."

I had an enormous family, friends, Geoff. I couldn't imagine being alone.

"On a different matter"—Mimi grinned—"Your mom wants to arrange an evening for you and her to drop by the Heron and do a taste-test."

I sighed in exasperation. I wanted a small, unassuming wedding next May when the lilacs were in bloom. Mom had a different idea, at least about the quiet, unassuming part, and she was out of control with extravagant wedding preparations. I mean, taste-testing? Now? The wedding was still nine months, four days—I glanced at the clock—and seven hours away. What was the hurry?

"Can't we hold off until after Hum Harbour Daze?"

She leaned back in her chair, stretching her feet under the table. "Keeping you busy, is it?"

"I had no idea volunteering to be on the Steering

Committee would turn into so much work."

"That's why I stepped down. Steering means organizing, organizing means supervising, and supervising is a euphemism for doing."

"How Carrie finds time to run her businesses, take care of her mother, and head up Hum Harbour Daze every year is beyond me."

"She's going to need help this year. The committee can't expect her to carry her usual load, not after what's just happened."

"I know. But I can't imagine who'd have the courage to step into her shoes."

Mimi nodded knowingly. A member of the Hunter clan had always headed Hum Harbour Daze. Always. The idea that anyone else might be in charge was tantamount to treason or something.

The kitchen phone rang. We both turned.

"Shouldn't you answer that?" Mimi asked. "It could be important."

"It goes to the machine after three rings. I figure Carrie can deal with them when she gets up."

"What if the call's for you?"

I hadn't thought of that.

"Check the call history."

I pushed a couple of buttons on the phone. "The calls came from the Inverness Arms."

"That's where Carrie's mother lives. How many times have they called?"

"According to the call history, four."

Mimi frowned. "Maybe something's wrong. You'd better answer the next time."

"And say what?"

"That Carrie can't come to the phone right now, but you will let her know as soon as possible."

I supposed I could handle that much.

Vi Murray was next to appear at the French door. The second ex-wife of local entrepreneur Ross Murray, Vi was our church secretary and privy to all the latest news. I ushered her into the kitchen and set her pie on the counter before accepting her embrace. It seemed I'd become the stand-in recipient of Carrie Hunter's sympathy hugs.

"Can you believe it?" she asked as she patted my back sympathetically. "A reporter's already called the church wanting background information for Claude's obituary.

"And I saw someone driving past Hunter Hall. Going slow, staring at the house, probably hoping to see something. This is going to bring the weird ones out of the woodwork."

I made a new pot of tea and listened to their speculations until the phone interrupted. The caller ID said Inverness Arms. With Mimi's nod, I picked up the receiver. I expected someone official. I got Carrie's mother.

"Where's my daughter?" asked Phyllis Hunter. I'd always been intimidated by the woman, and her strident voice had the same effect on me as fingernails on chalkboard. "And who are you?"

"Gailynn MacDonald, Mrs. Hunter. I'm sorry Carrie can't come to the phone right now." Mimi nodded encouragingly.

Mrs. Hunter sniffed. "That black MacDonald girl?" I assumed she referred to my hair color. "Anne MacDonald's daughter?"

"Yes, Mrs. Hunter. If you'd like to leave a message?"

Mimi cringed at my weak voice.

"No I don't want to leave a message. I want to talk to my daughter. Didn't your mother teach you any manners? Where's my daughter?"

"She can't come to the phone right now, Mrs. Hunter, but if you'd like to leave a message—"

"Don't Mrs. Hunter me, young lady. I should know better than to expect a straight answer from a MacDonald—"

"I'll make sure Carrie gets your message as soon as she's here."

"As soon as she's here? If she's not there, where is she? And why are you in my house?"

I glanced at Mimi for inspiration. "I'm on the Hum Harbour Daze Steering Committee with your daughter, Mrs. Hunter. She's upstairs right now. I can get her to call you as soon as she comes down." All true, though technically it didn't answer her questions. But it wasn't my place to tell this woman her house had been robbed, her son-in-law was dead, and her daughter was sleeping in a drugged stupor.

I held my breath.

"Well." Mrs. Hunter hmphed. "See that you do." And she hung up.

I poured myself a mug of strong tea and sank into the nearest chair.

"Sounds like Phyllis was in her usual form," Vi said.

I closed my eyes and swallowed scalding tea. Not that I was being a very good host, drinking in front of them. "Would either of you like some?"

Mimi declined. "I've been away from the café long enough." She hugged us both good-bye.

Vi, in no hurry to leave, accepted a frog mug full of tea, adding milk and sugar. "I can't get my mind around this. Just yesterday Claude told me he'd gotten his visa for Ghana. Not that you'd catch me running off to Africa."

"It's a gift, I think, to be able to leave everything you know and go someplace so different. Shows how much Carrie loved him."

"Oh, she wasn't going with him."

I sipped my tea and waited, knowing Vi would explain further.

"At least that's what Wee Claude told Reverend Innes. She couldn't go away and leave her mother alone."

"Which makes Claude's family estrangement so much sadder."

"I don't know anything about that, except I once overheard him telling the Reverend he'd had a terrible falling out with his father. He's never talked to anyone in his family since."

I wondered if Geoff knew more. It would be nice for Carrie if there was someone among Claude's family who could stay with her.

Vi was gone by the time Carrie padded into the kitchen. It was a quarter past noon. She'd twisted her hair back into a severe bun which, with her sedative-darkened eyes and pale complexion, only made her look more distant than ever. She seemed a little unsteady on her feet, so I held her arm and guided her into the closest chair.

I poured her tea. "Can I make you some lunch? Mimi and Vi dropped off a few things. You have a choice." I opened the fridge door and stood back so she could see.

"They brought all of that?"

"Mostly Mimi. Vi's pie is on the counter. And your

mother phoned." I didn't tell her how many times.

She cupped her mug between her hands as though she craved its warmth. "I'm not hungry, but I suppose I should eat something. Why don't you make lunch for both of us?"

"Both of us? I thought you might want to be alone."

Her lips started to quiver. "I'm going to be alone the rest of my life."

Afraid the tremor signaled another shrieking episode, I agreed without thinking. "Whatever you need—you just have to ask."

Which is how I ended up spending the night at Hunter Hall.

8

By day Hunter Hall was creepy, by night it was downright spooky. And having a forlorn basset hound glued to your heels didn't help. Caber was Claude's dog. I deduced from the uncertain way he and Carrie eyed each other, that although they might tolerate each other, they hadn't bonded. Which seemed odd, as I found Caber's humble charms endearing.

Until I tried sleeping with him, that is.

I was exhausted after the way Carrie'd kept me hopping the rest of the day. Go here, go there. Do this, do that. The woman needed an executive assistant, and trust me, I had no intentions of applying for the job. At some point in her privileged upbringing, Carrie's parents had apparently decided she didn't need to learn the words, thank you. Or, if she knew them, she didn't need to employ them. Apparently, thank you was what people said to them, not what they said to other people.

Hopefully, that wasn't how she'd treated Wee Claude.

Bone weary, I was looking forward to a good sleep.

Caber lay on my bed, his solid body pressed against the back of my legs. His wheeze rattled through the room, and I probably would have crammed the pillow over my head, except then I wouldn't hear Carrie.

Sometimes she cried in her sleep—not weeping, but she made these gasping sobs that sounded like weeping. At other times she wanted a sip of water. Or the simple assurance that she wasn't alone.

It didn't help that the day's heat culminated in a house-quaking thunderstorm. I don't usually mind storms. At home I'd open the curtains and pull my chair up to the window, waiting to see the lightning hit the water. It sizzled when it struck the sea. I loved that sound.

Unfortunately, my bedroom window at Hunter Hall faced the street. The street lights were out—as often happened during a storm—leaving nothing much to see. Or so I thought, until a flash illuminated the rain-slick pavement, and I spotted the man standing under the awning across the street. He had a tiny amber light that glowed intermittently—perhaps the tip of his cigarette when he inhaled? I half-hid behind my curtains, in case he could see me watching him watching Hunter Hall. He was still there when I gave up and crawled into bed.

By dawn's light Carrie had finally settled.

Unable to sleep, I dragged back the bedroom's heavy curtains and pushed open the windows to let in fresh morning air. I punched new life into my feather pillows and propped myself in bed to read. I'd scavenged the Bible from Claude's office.

I loved the story of Lazarus. I loved the way Jesus shared Mary and Martha's grief, and the way He loved them. So I flipped to John's Gospel, and sometime during my fourth read through the story, I conked out, too.

Caber's howling bark jarred me awake.

"Gailynn," Carrie shouted from across the hall, "I

am in the bath. Can you see who's at the front door?"

Ash hadn't packed a robe when she brought my overnight bag, so I wrapped the woven coverlet around my shoulders and raced down the stairs. In the echo-y old house my footfalls sounded like cannon fire.

Dear sweet brother Andrew, in uniform, and accompanied by an RCMP officer presumably from the Serious Crime Unit, stood on the front step. Andrew'd cupped his hands against the narrow glass window that edged the door and peered inside.

I unbolted the door and opened it a crack.

"Don't be a goof, Gai. Let us in. And if Carrie's awake, tell her Inspector LeClerc wants to see her." He reached out and patted down my hair, I guess to make me look more respectable.

"Do you want to wait in the kitchen? Or the parlor?"

Ignoring me, Andrew headed to the parlor, and the inspector, a vaguely attractive man of unassuming height, apologized for awakening me.

"Make yourself at home, and I'll tell Carrie you're here." Which they did, and I did, and in time—it appeared Carrie was not one to be rushed—she joined them in the parlor. Dressed, hair combed, and face scrubbed, I served them tea and breakfast scones, compliments of another neighbor.

Then I loitered in the next room and eavesdropped.

The last time we'd had a murder in Hum Harbour, the RCMP had remained in the background, while Andrew—with my assistance—identified the killer within a few days. From the tone of their voices, it seemed Andrew and the inspector considered Claude's death an accident. For form's sake, they asked the usual "Did your husband have any enemies?" and questioned her about Claude's competitive rivalries, like the one Claude shared with Danny-Boy Murdock.

When Carrie presented the insurance documents outlining the value of her missing frogs, however, I heard them shuffle to attention in their wing-backed chairs.

I'd pulled the files for Carrie the day before and almost fallen over myself when I read the price she'd paid for her folk art. I know people claim I charge an arm and a leg for my sea glass jewelry, but I, at least, use gold and silver. The frog figurines Carrie'd lost were molded porcelain. What's unique about that?

Inspector LeClerc cleared his throat. "Madame Oui," he said in Quebecois-accented English, "I assure you, we will resolve the investigation of your husband's death as soon as we can."

"Thank you," said Carrie. Apparently, RCMP Inspectors merited thanks.

They made rustling noises, as though preparing to leave.

"Madame Oui, your husband was a great Canadian. A great athlete. I promise you, if there is anything suspicious about his death, we will find it. We will see that justice is done."

I slipped into the kitchen as Carrie led them to the door. Their voices faded into an indiscernible mumble. Then Andrew popped into the kitchen.

"Gai, I almost forgot."

I pulled my head from the fridge, as though I'd just noticed him.

"Ash wanted me to tell you, she's closed Dunmaglass until you get back."

Dunmaglass was going to be famous one day. It

wasn't yet, of course. And it never would be if Ash closed the shop every time she had a whim. "What do you mean she's closed it?"

Andrew shrugged. "I dunno. She tried to explain but frankly, Gai, I'm a little preoccupied at the moment, so I didn't register what she was going on about. Maybe a trophy? That ring any bells?"

Carrie stood in the kitchen doorway. "The trophy? You mean the lobster boat trophy?" She'd commissioned a new trophy for Hum Harbour Daze's lobster boat races, and I'd agreed to display it in the front window at Dunmaglass.

She'd said the stained glass panels suspended in my front window, made by Helena Borgdenburger, were a perfect backdrop for the new trophy which was, coincidentally, created by Halbert Borgdenburger, her equally talented husband.

"Gailynn, if there's a problem with the trophy"—her voice cracked—"I can't bear another crisis. Please, you must go. I need you to solve whatever's wrong as soon as possible."

Andrew rejoined Inspector LeClerc at the front door and, having provided me with the reason to leave Hunter Hall, bid us good-bye.

"Are you sure you can manage without me?" I asked Carrie. "Do you want someone else to come over while I'm gone?"

"Don't worry about me, Gailynn. You're needed somewhere else. I understand completely."

"I'll be back once I sort things out."

"Not necessary. Really."

Her sudden willingness to see me gone, after twenty-four hours of seemingly endless demands, puzzled me, but I didn't argue. I dashed upstairs and crammed my stuff into my overnight bag while she watched me.

"You shouldn't be alone, Carrie. If you need me, call." I didn't linger over the offer, though. Instead, I exited Hunter Hall by the giant front door and booted it down the street to Dunmaglass and the disaster Ash considered worth closing my shop over.

9

Dunmaglass filled the main floor of the narrow one-hundred-fifty-year-old two-story stone building, which I owned. It was one of a string of similar buildings built hip to jowl along Hum Harbour's narrow Main Street. Named after a local Scottish settlement that disappeared long ago, Dunmaglass specialized in my own one-of-a-kind sea glass jewelry, a local artist's blown glass vases and sculptures, and his wife's dramatically placed stained glass panels, also for sale, although no one had ever offered to buy one.

I didn't mind, and neither did Helena Borgdenburger, their creator. The panels had gained her a well-deserved reputation throughout Atlantic Canada; corporations and churches commissioned her work after seeing the panels in my shop. While inside Dunmaglass ooohing over Helena's work, these people also purchased pieces of my jewelry and/or her husband's creations. So it was what one might call a win-win situation.

A giant, multi-paned bay window fronted Dunmaglass. It was the perfect display location for my favorite stained glass panels—the lighthouse on the rocks at the end of the harbor.

Carrie's new lobster boat trophy was supposed to sit on the curved stone sill in front of the stained glass where the whole world could see it and, hopefully, inspire a few more racers to join the Hum Harbour

Daze competition.

As I approached the shop, I noted duct tape over cardboard replaced five of the square window panes. Not a good sign.

Hands trembling, I fitted my key into the door lock, and let myself into the shop. The tiny bell over the door jingled. A year ago my shop had been vandalized. Since then I'd installed a security system, but my stomach still clenched when I remembered the destruction.

Squeezing my eyes shut, I said a silent prayer. I fisted my hands and braced myself for the worst. Then I flipped on the lights.

The perfectly normal shop displays stole my breath. I sagged against the doorframe in relief.

"Ash? Ash, are you here?" Her footfalls pounded down the stairs, and she looked neither concerned, nor frazzled, when she emerged into the open.

"Hey, Gai," she said with a smile. "You came."

"Of course I came. Andrew said there'd been a disaster at the shop and—"

"D-disaster? Is that what he told you?"

"He didn't remember exactly what you'd said, but yes, disaster was the general drift of it."

She hurried forward, and gave me a big hug. I guess I looked like I needed one. "It's OK. Everything's OK. R-really."

"Then what happened to my window? And where's the new trophy? Don't tell me it's broken. Or stolen. It's not missing, is it?" I couldn't keep new panic from my voice.

The trophy was a Halbert Borgdenburger original—a replica of a Northumberland lobster boat, dusted in sea spray as it crested a frothy wave—all in blown glass, mounted on a polished, Birdseye maple pedestal. Spectacular. Irreplaceable.

Nowhere in sight.

"It's upstairs," Ash said. "When I came in to work this morning and found the b-busted windows I was, like, 'that trophy's not safe down here, especially with the window guys coming this afternoon.' So I locked it in your office room. Well, shut it in the office, I d-didn't lock the door 'cause you can't, and Sheba doesn't open doors."—Sheba's my cat—"But I figured you wouldn't want her around the trophy in c-case she, like, brushed against it and knocked it over or something."

I placed a steadying hand over my thumping heart and took a deep breath. "Do you know what actually happened to the window?"

She shrugged. "K-kids, I guess. I couldn't see anyone on the video feed. They kept out of range of the camera."

I remembered that unsettling moment the previous night, when I saw someone watching Hunter Hall. It seemed hard to believe that someone else was outside in last night's storm. "How am I supposed to catch vandals I can't see?"

She didn't seem concerned by this injustice. "I called the window repair guy."

"And you thought it was best to close the shop until they finished working?"

She tilted her head, considering. "Yeah."

I had put her in charge.

"But the rest of the store is OK?"

She slapped my shoulder a little too enthusiastically for my comfort. "Everything's g-great."

No disaster, just a small calamity. I smiled with relief. As was so often the case, Andrew'd gotten it wrong. "Then I guess we can reopen."

"Before you d-do, maybe could you come upstairs for a minute?"

I think that's when I registered that Sheba hadn't greeted me in her usual, enthusiastic way. Had I relaxed too soon?

"What's wrong?"

"Nothing's wrong. N-not here. But it c-could be…"

Ash's stammer intensified when something was amiss. And there was no point waiting for her to work her way through an explanation. You could solve six murders before she ever got there. So I checked that the shop was still locked and led the way to my upstairs apartment.

Apart from the large black cat trying to cram herself into a gift-bag in the middle of my living room floor—she did not fit—and the kitchen frog strategically placed in the middle of my coffee table, the place looked fine.

Ash pointed at the frog.

Frankly, after spending the last twenty-four hours surrounded by Carrie Hunter's ridiculous frog collection, I wasn't particularly thrilled to find another ceramic amphibian center-stage in my own home.

"Mom's kitchen frog," I said. "What about it?"

"You recognize it?"

I am not on a first name basis with the neighborhood kitchen do-dads, but I was pretty sure this was my mother's. I'd never seen another painted Nova Scotia tartan.

"You found Mom's frog."

"It was g-given to me."

"By whom?" I felt required to ask.

"Josh."

Josh Pry, Ash's boyfriend.

"He found a tartan frog like Mom's and gave it to you? That's nice, I guess."

She tore off a strip of fingernail with hcr teeth. "Not like your m-mom's. This one is your m-mom's."

I picked it up, turned it over, recognized the telltale chip from when my brother, Andrew, had pitched it at my other brother, Sam. There'd been a corresponding lump on the back of Sam's head, as I recalled.

"Where did he find it? Did he say?"

"He probably d-didn't think I'd recognize it. I mean, how many people are into frogs like I am?"

"Carrie Hunter?" I muttered.

Ash seemed too distressed to hear. "What should I do? Give it back? T-tell him to give it back? And what about all the other f-frogs he's given me?"

"Other frogs?" Oh dear.

"Every week a new one. Or a d-different one? What if he stole them all?"

I flopped down on my floral couch. Not in its usual ponytail, my hair spilled annoyingly into my face. What if Josh was Hum Harbour's frog thief? What if he was the one who'd absconded with Carrie's precious figurines? Worse still, what if Josh had killed Claude Oui in the midst of the robbery?

I could tell by the look on Ash's face that she hadn't connected the dots. She didn't know about Carrie's collection, or its missing pieces, or that Claude's death was anything more than a tragic accident.

I didn't actually know that, either.

What I did know was that Josh's frog stealing days were over. And obviously, since Ash had only told me and no one else about her suspicions—"Have you told anyone else?"

She shook her head.

She wanted me to deal with this as quickly and quietly as possible. Which was also why she'd closed Dunmaglass, she explained. I needed to confront Josh.

"Why me?" I asked.

"He likes you. He's fishing with his dad. B-But when he gets back tonight, can you talk to him?"

Dunmaglass faces Main Street, but my back windows overlook the harbor. I could see the fleet was gone for the day. That gave me a few hours to decide how I'd confront him. Although Ash didn't realize it, we were talking about a bigger crime than lifting a few kitchen frogs.

Josh might be involved in Claude's death

"Until then, we may as well open Dunmaglass. Can you handle it?"

She nodded again.

"Then off you go." I made shooing motions with my hands. "I'm going to shower and change and head to the clinic. Geoff gave me yesterday off. I don't want to miss today too, if I can help it."

As soon as she disappeared, I flopped sideways on the couch. The disaster I'd anticipated—a smashed one-of-a-kind trophy—had turned out to be nothing more serious than a couple of broken window panes. I'd call the security company and have them readjust the cameras to cover more than Dunmaglass's front and back doors. The secondary disaster, however, the one I'd walked into without warning, was much worse.

Ash's boyfriend was a thief. A thief with a thing for frogs.

With Claude Oui dead and Carrie missing a few of her own prize amphibians, it looked as though Ash's beau had become the prime suspect.

10

I am a medical receptionist. I say this with pride, the way Evie Carnahan declares, "I am a librarian" to Rick O'Connell, in the movie, *The Mummy*. I also have long, black hair, but that's where the likeness ends. Her eyes are green, mine are hazel. She's tall—five-seven—I'm small in comparison—five-four on a good day. She has a delightful British accent, and I speak plain, old, Canadian.

We do share another important thing, though. We both have amazingly handsome sidekicks who help us solve mysteries.

My comrade-in-arms is the breathtakingly dashing Dr. Geoffrey Grant, my employer and fiancé. He took over Doc Campbell's practice last spring when Doc retired. Within days, Doc was dead—murdered—and Geoff and I were determined to catch his killer. OK, I was determined to catch the killer, and Geoff was determined to keep me out of trouble. His task proved harder than mine, though not as heartbreaking. You see, Doc's murderer was my life-long best friend.

I had no idea how to cope with the devastating discovery, but after five years as a missionary in Somalia, Geoff was well versed in coping with loss. He understood, he listened, he held me when I cried, and it seemed only natural to fall in love with him. Unavoidable, really. And I am so thankful God could bring something this good out of a situation that was that bad.

When I arrived at the clinic, it was regular Wednesday busy, which meant steady, but not frenetic. Geoff and I worked well together and had achieved a kind of rapport I never managed with his predecessor, Doc Campbell. We understood how each other's minds worked and could anticipate what the other wanted, or needed, in order to do our jobs well.

So, by four-thirty I was closing the file on the day's last patient and sending the required billing statement off to Nova Scotia Health for payment.

Geoff leaned against the doorframe, watching me log off the computer. "Got dinner plans?" he asked. We often shared meals.

"I promised Ash I'd talk to Josh once he got back."

"That's not until sunset." When the boats came in.

"So, dinner at your place or mine?" I asked.

"Why don't I cook? I bet you're worn a little thin after last night with Carrie Hunter."

He had no idea.

"We'll eat at six. Gives us time to hit the beach before you go."

Morning and night, I walked the beach scavenging for sea glass. I wasn't always successful, but I loved the routine. I followed Geoff out of the clinic, and after he locked the door, we walked home.

Hum Harbour is a small fishing village along the rugged shores of Cape George, Nova Scotia. Its four main streets parallel the shoreline's curve, each one riding higher up the steep hillside. Water Street, with the wharf, fish plant, and Bait 'N Tackle, was closest to the harbor. Main Street, where I live, housed the business section. The clinic was on Pictou Street, and uppermost, Murray Street, connected to the highway.

Geoff lived next door to Dunmaglass, in the apartment above my cousin's Hubris Heron Seafood Café.

"I saw your broken windows this morning," he said as Dunmaglass came into view.

"Did you hear any commotion last night? Ash said it was probably kids, but I'm worried."

"That you'll have another break-in?"

I shoved the unpleasant suggestion to the back of my mind. "Have you seen anyone lurking around?"

Geoff draped his arm across my shoulders. "You're letting your imagination run away with you, Gai. Don't let Claude's accident spook you."

"How can you be so sure it was an accident?"

"Gai."

"Hear me out. Carrie's robbed. Claude's killed. My windows are broken. There was someone watching Hunter Hall last night. Don't you find all that suspicious?"

His arm stiffened when I mentioned the late-night watcher. "Could you see who it was?"

"The street lights were out in the storm. But what if it was the thief? Or the murderer? What if they're one and the same?"

The clefts in his cheeks deepened when he pressed his lips together. Usually that meant he was struggling to find the right words. Right now, his right words would be telling me to drop the whole thing.

I didn't want to hear that.

Geoff surprised me, though. "If you know something you need to tell Andrew."

Not before I'd made sure my suspicions had merit. "But what if I'm wrong? You know how I get carried away." We stopped in front of Dunmaglass. Clear window glass replaced the duct tape and cardboard squares. Not the warped antique glass that used to fill the panes, but a definite improvement on the duct tape.

Geoff cupped my face between his hands and kissed me soundly. "Then promise me you'll leave this to Andrew." He looked so earnest and concerned; I wondered if he'd include my promise to confront Josh about stealing among the things I should leave to Andrew.

"Does that include me talking to the frog thief?"

"Do you know who your frog thief is?"

"I think so. Maybe. Probably. Yes."

"You'd already decided to confront him yourself?"

"We could go together, if you want. We'd just talk to him."

"Gai."

"Is there any harm in that?"

"Tonight, I suppose?" Geoff, always two steps ahead of me, realized I was talking about my impending chat with Josh. "You were going to do it without me."

"I don't need your permission to talk to people, you know."

Geoff peered into my eyes, as if trying to see through to my brain, and decipher what was in there. "You should. Especially if you're going to start accusing them of murder."

I pulled away. "What do you think I am? Some brainless ninny who flies off half-cocked every time I turn around?" I poked his chest for emphasis.

"I'm not the one who sees a murderer under every bush."

"And you think I do?"

"Don't you?"

"Kitchen frogs. All I'm going to talk about is kitchen frogs!" I flung open the door to Dunmaglass, almost knocking the bell off its hinge. "If the topic of murder comes up, trust me, I won't be the one to blame."

"It won't be anyone else."

Angered by his lack of trust, too stubborn to admit Geoff might be right, I stomped through to my apartment.

As usual, Sheba sat in the middle of the table, waiting for supper. My moods didn't bother her. As long as she had her kibble, I could rant and rave to my heart's content.

Which I did.

11

I had a small deck above Dunmaglass's back storeroom. There was just enough room for a couple of chairs and a potted palm, which lived inside my apartment ten months of the year. Geoff had a larger deck over the Hubris Heron's kitchen. Since less than a foot of space separates Dunmaglass from the Heron, Geoff built a small bridge so we wouldn't have to walk downstairs, outside, and upstairs again to reach each other.

By the time I crossed the connector, any negative feelings I might have harbored had dissipated in the fervor of romantic anticipation.

Geoff'd set his outside table with a hand-me-down tablecloth, mismatched china, and old cutlery he'd picked up at the thrift shop. A mason jar overflowed with cone flowers, bee balm, and daisies that quivered shyly in the breeze. Since our second-storey decks overlooked the wharf, it could be idyllic or deafening, depending on the time of day and the amount of activity below. At the moment, things were still quiet. However, I could see the first of the fishing fleet rounding the breakwater as they chugged home.

Geoff wore an apron around his trim waist. He kissed my cheek before setting wooden bowls of salad at each place, and we took our seats. As always, we held hands while he prayed, and I confess, I didn't close my eyes. I loved to watch the way our hands looked with his long, perpetually-tanned fingers linked protectively through mine and the way my diamond ring—once his mom's—magically caught the late afternoon sun, spinning tiny stars of light against the underside of his patio umbrella. Another bargain store find.

Risotto followed salad. Fruit and custard—compliments of the Hubris Heron and cousin Mimi—followed the risotto.

We ate and talked and kissed and absently watched Josh and his dad off-load the day's catch. Neither of us felt keen about ending our dinner, much less confronting Josh regarding his frog thefts. Geoff would come with me—whether to keep me in line or keep Josh out of trouble should he fail to keep me in line--I wasn't sure. But any excuse to have Geoff near was good.

Darkness came too early in August, when the air still sagged with summer heat, and no one wanted to head indoors for the night. A couple of years ago, colored patio lights were all the rage, and it seemed like everyone in town bought strings of plastic lanterns. As Geoff and I walked to Ash's house to meet Josh, we could see the colorful lights in every backyard along the way. Voices and tantalizing BBQ fragrances wafted from all directions.

We found Ash and Josh entwined on the front step of her parents' two-story. When Geoff cleared his throat they unfurled, arms and legs detangling, two bodies emerging from one mass. They reminded me of the poppies in my mom's garden, the way their enormous blossoms swell once the tiny pods burst.

"I hope we haven't kept you waiting," I said, knowing we had given Josh a mere twenty minutes to get home, shower, change, and drive the quarter mile to Ash's house.

She smoothed her strawberry blonde hair, evidently unaware of the state of her t-shirt. "Josh just g-got here," she said.

Geoff squeezed in between the two, wriggling his hips back and forth to create enough space to sit. "And I understand you have something to tell us." He fixed Josh with his most impenetrable stare.

I know I can never resist it.

Josh poked at the do-rag he wore over cornrows. His headgear had caused quite a stir when he first donned it.

"That kid's wearing a hairnet!" was the most common comment. A few thought it marked Josh as the local drug dealer—cheap advertising. They worried that once the police figured this out, Josh would get arrested and his dad would lose a good fishing hand. I even heard one lady suggest the kindest thing would be for the community to chip in and help his parents pay for therapy. A boy with that serious a case of germaphobia needed professional help.

According to Ash, though, the do-rag was simply a step in Josh's continuing research into his African-Canadian heritage.

Personally, I was surprised to learn do-rags were traditional for anyone but gangbangers, but what could I say? Apparently, my ancestors painted themselves blue.

Judging by the way Josh now plucked at the thin fabric as we awaited his answer, his headgear had become uncomfortably tight. "Ash's like, 'You have to tell.'" He ran his gaze across the three of us. "But I'm like, who's gonna care? They're just kitchen frogs."

"That's not the point."

He'd worked his index finger under the mesh and scratched his scalp. "My mom made herself one in ceramics class. She took this night school course, you know? Cost her, like, five bucks for the greenware and firing."

Ash folded her arms across her chest. "Did you give me her f-frog, too?"

"Babe, I did it for you."

"For me?" Ash thrust out her lower lip, and Josh's shoulders curled inward. Surely a murderer couldn't be so easily rebuked.

"You want me to give 'em back?"

Geoff asked, "What do you think?"

Forget kitchen frogs, I was more concerned with the bigger picture. "Did you take any frogs from Hunter Hall?"

"Are you kidding? That place gives me the creeps." He said it with such conviction, I believed him. It gave me the creeps, too.

12

Tide was low and the moon was high by the time Geoff and I ambled hand-in-hand along the shore. Soft, lapping waves whispered across the gravel. I found a couple of pieces of white sea glass—white reflects moonlight better than colored glass, which looks pebble black at night.

Geoff's thoughts seemed far away, but I was glad to finally have him to myself.

"Are you still thinking about Josh?"

He glanced at me, as though surprised to find me attached to his hand. "Not really."

I tried to look encouraging and waited for him to elaborate.

"Not at all, actually." He stooped to pick up a stone and tossed it into the water. "I can't get Claude out of my mind."

I slid my arms around his waist and hugged him tight. "It wasn't your fault."

"I'm not so sure. Ever since Danny-Boy Murdock lost control of his hammer and whacked Claude in the head, I'd been telling Claude to be careful. He couldn't afford another serious head injury."

"But you yourself said this bump wasn't serious."

"Obviously I was wrong. Either I misdiagnosed Claude's initial injury, which was worse than I thought, and I should have insisted he quit competition immediately. Or that silly tussle with

Murdock and the bump Claude got when he fell was worse than I thought, and I should have insisted he go to Emergency and get checked by a specialist."

"Claude was a big boy. If he refused to follow your expert medical advice there was nothing you could do."

He rested his cheek against the top of my head. "Then why do I feel so guilty?"

"Because you are a wonderful, loving man who cares about people. And besides, there's still the question about whether or not Claude took that tumble under his own steam."

Geoff pulled away. "Don't."

"He could have slipped on that loose stair runner. He was unsteady on his feet, sometimes."

"Which I should have taken into consideration."

"But it's also possible someone sneaked into the house after you left and whacked Claude over the head while stealing Carrie's frogs. Maybe the guy I saw hanging around outside Hunter Hall."

"Gai, didn't you learn anything the last time you decided someone had been murdered?"

"After what happened to Doc, we both know we can't dismiss the possibility of foul play without at least considering it."

"Yes, we can." He took me by the shoulders, bent his face level with mine. "I've already told you, I won't have you storming around town upsetting everyone with some wild hypothesis about what happened."

"Some wild hypothesis?" I choked on the words. How could Geoff show such limited appreciation of how much I'd matured since he'd come into my life? The way he dismissed the wisdom I'd gained since my last murder investigation ignited my indignation.

Fists on hips, nose to nose, we faced each other, unmindful of the shifting tide advancing toward our feet.

"I would never do such a thing!"

"Yes, you would. You like the idea that someone pushed Claude down the stairs. It excites you."

"How could you think that?"

"I just have to look at you—the way your eyes shine whenever the idea of a crime pops into your head."

I stepped back a pace. "How do you know what pops into my head?"

"You aren't that complicated."

He might have meant that as a positive trait, but I sure didn't take it that way. My face burned with fury at being dismissed as, as..."Simple minded? Are you saying I'm simple minded?"

His jaw dropped open.

"Because I'll have you know I am not simple. I am complicated. And multifaceted. And unique. And... complicated."

"Gai—"

"And I am not some sadistic weirdo who gets off on other peoples' misery."

"I didn't say—"

"And furthermore—" I suddenly noticed the water licking at my ankles, and heart thundering, I leaped up the beach faster than a sand flea on speed. "I was only trying to make you feel better because whatever happened to Claude was not your fault!"

"Gai—"

"But far be it from me, a simple medical receptionist, to suggest I might know better than the mighty doctor whether or not he's to blame for someone dying on his watch."

He caught my elbow, but I shook off his hand.

"Go ahead and blame yourself if it makes you feel better." I marched towards the wharf. "I sure won't stop you!"

I don't know what he did after that.

OK. Technically, I do.

13

Less than thirty minutes later Geoff stood on my back deck, flowers in hand, knocking on the frame of the open sliding door. My outside light wasn't on, but I could see him, his head bowed humbly, in the pool of living room light that spread across the deck.

I left him there for a quarter of a heartbeat—I didn't want to seem too eager to forgive him—before inviting him inside.

He held out the splendid bouquet that had adorned his dinner table. "I'm sorry."

I flew into his arms, burying my tear-stained face against his chest. "So. Am. I."

He held me tight as the moisture from the dripping flower stems soaked through my shirt. Pleasantly refreshed, at first, I eventually pulled free and found a vase. I set the flowers in the middle of my table and thanked Geoff appropriately.

It was a silly argument anyway, which didn't deserve that second run through after the afternoon's set-to. I changed into a dry top, and we settled on the couch.

One of the things I enjoyed about my apartment was its privacy. The only entrances were through the shop and the tiny bridge Geoff made between his deck and mine. If I didn't want company I could pretty much guarantee no company.

Geoff, of course, was the exception. He was always

welcome.

He and I snuggled and kissed and briefly discussed whether he'd prefer white gold or yellow for his wedding band. All very delightful, really, until the tiny hairs on my arms began to prickle. And not in a good way.

I opened my eyes and shifted so I could peer over his shoulder. From that position, I could see the darkness of my unlit deck. (We'd dimmed my apartment lights for a more romantic atmosphere, leaving no excess light flowing from the living room.)

Two faces—one pale, the other so dark all I could make out were the teeth—pressed against my sliding glass door. I almost had a heart attack.

Geoff reacted instantly. Perhaps having someone shriek in your ear does that to you.

He sprang to his feet, vaulted the coffee table, and flung the glass door wide.

The prowlers stood with mouths gaping. I guess they hadn't expected my reaction, either.

"What in creation do you think you're doing?!" Geoff bellowed as he hauled Josh inside by his t-shirt. Ash, her arm wrapped tight around Josh's waist, staggered in with him.

They sputtered in unison.

"How did you get up there in the first place?" I wanted to know.

Josh regained his composure first. "Easy. We sneaked up the back stairs at the Heron, through Geoff's place to the back deck, and across to yours."

"You broke into Geoff's apartment?"

Ash's eyes widened innocently. "We d-didn't break in. The door was open. We called, but you guys didn't answer so we came here."

"Cool bridge," said Josh.

"Thanks," said Geoff.

"Don't change the subject. You can't just let yourself into someone's house when they're not home, even if the door's unlocked."

No one in Hum Harbour locked their doors. People came and went as they pleased. Need a cup of sugar? Ask your neighbor. Your neighbor's not home? Help yourself. They won't mind. It was the basic neighbors' code in these parts. We all knew it. And we all knew that it was the scare, not the crime, that made me react so strongly. Maybe crime wasn't the right word.

"Now that you're here," I said. "What do you want?"

Ash elbowed Josh in the ribs. "Josh has something to say."

Geoff and I turned on him—perhaps I should rephrase. We turned to him.

"Ash says I have to tell you I was outside Hunter Hall the other night. You know, when everything happened."

"The night Claude died?"

Geoff stiffened. "You saw what happened?"

Josh looked to Ash for support. "Sorta. I mean, I was there, and I saw you, like, talking with Claude." He stuffed his hands into the front pockets of his low-slung jeans, perhaps to keep himself from nervously scratching his head. "And I saw Danny-Boy Murdock bust in and leave again."

"What were you doing there?" Geoff asked.

Josh's hands reappeared. He held them up I-surrender style. "I just happened by."

"And hung around for a bit."

"Yeah, well, I heard shouting and I'm, like, maybe I should hang around in case someone needs me." He apparently considered that a reasonable explanation.

"So while all this shouting was happening, you hung out where, exactly?"

"Ah..." I could see the wheels in his head trying to turn. "On the sidewalk?"

Hunter Hall was built right smack-dab up to the sidewalk, but I wasn't sure you could hear what was happening in the middle of the house—no matter how loud it got.

My dearest Geoff, who always gives everyone the benefit of the doubt, said, "I don't think you're being entirely truthful with us."

Josh's face looked as forlorn as Caber's. "I knew you wouldn't believe me, but Ash was like, 'of course they will. They're Christians. They have to believe what we say.'"

"Only if it's true," said Geoff.

"Well it is. I went to help, but you didn't need me, so then I left."

"What time did you leave?" I asked.

"I don't wear a watch, but," he rushed on before I could accuse him of making excuses, "I followed Danny-Boy out to make sure he didn't circle back."

"While you were doing that, did you happen to notice anyone else, or see anything suspicious?"

Josh scratched under his do-rag. "Like what?"

"Someone standing across the street?"

He studied the ceiling. Maybe he was replaying the evening in his head. Maybe he was trying to come up with a plausible answer, though I had no idea why he'd lie. Unless, of course, he'd been lying all along.

"I didn't see nobody but me and Danny-Boy."

"Thank you for your honesty," said Geoff.

Honesty, shmonesty. How could he believe Josh? Why didn't I?

14

I let Ash and Josh out the official way, through the downstairs door, and double locked it after them.

Geoff departed via our deck bridge.

Sheba was out prowling for the night, so I locked my sliding glass door, too. I didn't normally lock it, but tonight I was feeling vulnerable, and the security of a locked door went a long way to quelling my uneasiness.

The air was heavy. I left my window wide open, floral curtains drawn back in case a breeze erupted during the night—it usually did—and then stretched out on top of my covers.

The last two days had been distressing, and although I was super-tired, I couldn't stop my brain from spinning. I relived every detail from the moment I heard Carrie scream, trying to make sense of something that made no sense at all.

Who would wish Claude Oui harm? I knew there was that feud between Wee Claude and Danny-Boy, but it was just a publicity stunt. Wasn't it? He hadn't really meant to hurt Claude the day his hammer flew out of control and clobbered Claude. It had been a dreadful accident. Hadn't it?

As for Josh and his thieving ways—they were equally innocent, weren't they? Just a teenaged boy's misguided attempt to romance the girl of his dreams. Though I had to admit he was pretty good at creeping up undetected. He was pretty good at lying, too. Was he telling the truth when he said he'd followed Danny-Boy to make sure he didn't double back? Come to think of it, we never asked Josh if he doubled back, himself.

The breeze arrived, caressing my skin, reminding me of another's caresses.

Was Geoff right? Did I secretly yearn for the excitement of another murder investigation?

OK, according to him it wasn't secret. But was he right? Did I long for the thrill of another murder in our sleepy little village—like some kind of warped change-of-pace? Was I really that insensitive? Tears ran down the side of my face into my ear.

Claude. Poor Claude. Who could do such a thing? Poor Carrie. What was she going to do, alone in that great big house?

What if one day I woke up and found Geoff dead at the bottom of the stairs? What would I do? My tears flowed harder, and I curled into a ball around my pillow.

By morning, I was in a different frame of mind.

****

Everything irked me. Sheba, stinking of rotten fish guts, had apparently passed the entire night in a garbage bin. My apartment was a mess. I'd bedded down for the night without my usual straightening-up nightcap. Filling my coffee pot and setting the timer was perhaps the most important part of that nightly routine, and I'd neglected that, too. Geoff's flowers hung over the side of the vase like a limp curtain. And, to top it off, I was out of conditioner.

I stood in the shower, soapy suds in my eyes, and roared like a lion. Geoff said my hazel eyes reminded him of the cubs in Somalia—although I'm not sure whether he actually saw lions in Somalia or somewhere else while he was in Africa.

My morning plan was to head for work early enough to stop by Andrew's and get the heads-up on the Claude Oui investigation. I did not want the police entertaining any hint that Geoff was in any way responsible for Claude's death. He had done all due diligence as Claude's doctor, and if Claude was too macho to tell Carrie he'd banged his head again…besides, what kind of man left a loose carpet rod on the stairs? An accident waiting to happen and, again, not Geoff's fault.

In the process of talking things through with Andrew, I'd include what I knew about fast-fingered Josh. Investigating my last murder, I learned the hard way the consequences of trying to handle things on my own. Claude's death was a police matter. I had to leave it with them, and if Josh was involved, even coincidentally, it would be wrong for me to hide that information from Andrew.

Before facing my brother, though, I needed coffee.

Geoff always had a fresh pot brewing. He was leaning against the counter, reading his morning paper when I tapped on his kitchen window.

"Have mercy on a coffee-less soul?" I asked when he looked up in surprise. "I forgot to fill my pot before I went to bed."

He clicked his tongue in compassion as I let myself in. "Disastrous state of affairs." Taking a clean mug from the dish rack in his sink, he filled it with his extra strong blend, leaving enough room for milk and sugar.

"I was hoping to see Andrew before we opened the clinic," I said. "See if he has any news."

"There won't be anything yet. You know how notoriously long it takes for any reports to come in."

"But maybe he's found something in the evidence they took away."

He studied me over the rim of his mug. "I thought you were going to leave the investigation to the police?"

"Andrew needs to know about Josh—what he said about following Danny-Boy after his argument with Claude."

"Andrew'll be up to his ears today interviewing whoever else he thinks might know something. He kept me for almost two hours yesterday."

"You?" Visions of Geoff handcuffed to a steel chair in a skuzzy interrogation room filled my head, even though I knew Hum Harbour's miniscule police station didn't have an interrogation room. Or a jail cell. It was basically a one-room cottage divided into an outer office and closet-sized inner office.

"Yes, me. Then Danny-Boy Murdock. He'll probably want to see you, today."

"Me?"

"You were with Carrie from the moment she found Claude. You could have heard or noticed something that seemed insignificant at the time." He set down his mug with a clunk. "Wipe the stars out of your eyes, Gai."

I tried. Really I did. "When am I supposed to be questioned?"

"We'll open the clinic this morning as usual. I've only got a couple of appointments booked so it shouldn't be busy. Whenever he does call, you can slip away."

I sipped my coffee.

Andrew's interviews could drag on and on, as Geoff's two-hour chat confirmed. Surely, at some point during our conversation I'd be able to milk my brother for information on the investigation's progress. "Then I'll tell Andrew about Josh. And the guy I saw watching Hunter Hall."

****

Geoff had two booked appointments, but he was always available for minor emergencies—such as Elliot Macintosh. The seven-year-old one-man-disaster-master and his mom arrived while Geoff was seeing his first patient. She'd already stabilized Elliot's injured arm in a sling. I checked his fingers as Geoff had taught me; they were warm to the touch and moved easily despite their shocking black-and-purple coloration. He could wait a few minutes for treatment—sort of.

The last time Elliot had been stuck in the waiting room for more than ten minutes, he'd tried scaling the magazine rack, and, by the time he actually saw Geoff, he was in worse shape than when he arrived. So was Kimmy Thomlinson, whom Elliot—and the rack—had fallen on.

I fit Elliot into the next time slot and explained to Geoff's second appointment that the doctor was running a little behind schedule. Knowing Elliot, as everyone does, Geoff's second appointment approved the shift.

Sissy Sinclair and babies Bobby and Becky arrived as I ushered Elliot and his mom into Geoff's examination room. Sissy's six-month-old twins required more paraphernalia than a professional hockey team, so her mom accompanied them everywhere. The babies slumbered silently in their double stroller, belying Sissy's claim they'd come down with a severe case of whooping cough overnight.

The digital ear thermometer indicated neither babe was fevered, so I let them wait, too. Sissy and her mom sank into the waiting room's padded chairs, and the next time I looked up Sissy was sound asleep, her head against her mom's shoulder. I guess she needed a good sleep as much as her kids.

The clock on the wall ticked softly.

Sissy's mom flipped pages of a magazine.

Geoff's second appointment angled his chair so he could watch the sleeping babies.

Andrew did not call.

I looked up Post Concussion Syndrome on the Internet. I wanted to know the signs, symptoms, and treatments, so the next time Geoff said he'd not done enough for Claude, I could point out what the experts said and how he'd followed all of their recommendations to a T. I didn't have to check Claude's medical records to confirm that. I knew Geoff, and I knew he'd leave nothing to chance with Claude. Or any other patient. That's the way Geoff is.

If necessary, of course, I'd have Claude's chart on hand to prove this fact to Geoff and whoever else might ask. Like Andrew.

I'd gotten as far as symptoms: headaches, irritability, noise and light sensitivity, when the mail arrived. Regretfully, I set aside my research and went back to work. I never did get back to it.

****

Andrew sat behind the desk in the police station's closet-like inner office, looking all spit-and-polish and official. For the past few years, he'd been working his way through the RCMP's entrance requirements, and this chance to work with their Serious Crime Unit was a big deal for him. He wanted all Inspector LeClerc's impressions—first, last, and in between—to be favorable.

Being the loving sister I was, I wanted to do my best to facilitate the process—as long as it coincided with my own agenda, which was protecting Geoff. I figured informing on Josh Pry fell within that category, too.

As best I could, I answered questions like, "Where were you when you first heard Carrie Hunter call for help? What did you see when you entered the house? How would you describe Carrie's frame of mind?" I wavered a bit at, "While you spent the evening and night with Carrie, did you, or she, notice anything else missing?"

"No, but I did see—"

Andrew raised his hand. "Don't volunteer irrelevant theories I don't need. Don't tell me anything I haven't specifically asked about."

"But—"

"Do you understand?"

One of the things that annoyed me most about Andrew was me. The way I folded whenever he challenged me. So he was older. So he had a college degree. So he'd become a successful police officer with commendations under his belt.

I was successful, too.

I stood, bracing my hands on the edge of his desk and leaned in. LeClerc, who was working in the outer office, didn't need to hear what I had to say, just Andrew.

Sucking in a deep breath for courage—I'd never stood up to my brother before—I said through gritted teeth, "Do *you* understand? Because that's the bigger question."

"Keep out of this, Gai."

"Only after I tell you Josh Pry steals kitchen frogs."

"He what?"

"I don't care what you do with that information, but you need to know." I turned on my heels, and, chin held high, walked out.

I felt so proud I almost high-fived myself.

Outside the station, Carrie Hunter sat in her SUV. She'd cranked the windows down to catch the breeze blowing off the water. We might be four blocks uphill from the shore but the wind was strong enough to lift my ponytail and tug at my skirt.

It'd been over twenty-four hours since I'd last seen her, and it didn't look like she'd slept a wink in the interim. Big, dark glasses hid half her face. The parts I could see sagged with weariness.

I rested my elbows on the car's open window, not sure what to say that didn't sound corny, and winged a silent prayer heavenward. *Lord, strengthen her.*

"I'm glad I found you," Carrie said. "I drove by the clinic. Geoff told me you'd be here."

She came looking for me?

"Your brother grilled me for over an hour." She pushed up her glasses and dabbed her eyes with tissue. "I guess he didn't really grill me. I'm just so tired, it felt like a grilling."

"Is there anything I can do?"

"I was hoping you'd say that. Claude's memorial service is tomorrow. They told me I couldn't have his body until the police are done with it, but..." She blew her nose. I noticed the wad of used tissues on the seat beside her. "I need to do this now. I can't wait on the police."

I reached in the window and squeezed her hand.

"The thing is, we have another meeting tonight." She meant the Hum Harbour Daze Steering Committee. "And I don't know if I'll be able to handle it."

"Why don't you get someone else to chair?"

"Oh, would you, Gailynn? I don't know if I'll be in any condition to decide who'll take Claude's place as parade marshal."

International Highland Heavyweight Champion Wee Claude was supposed to preside over Hum Harbour Daze's big parade, and ride the lobster float with the festival queen. It had been planned for months. I had no idea who'd be considered an acceptable alternative.

"Carrie, this is my first year on the committee. I don't think I'd be very good at chairing."

"Of course you would. You don't have an agenda like most of the other committee members. I can trust you to handle the discussion fairly."

Summer weather in Nova Scotia is known for its changeability, and the wind took on a sudden chill. Or maybe it was just me feeling chilled at the thought of what she asked. But I couldn't think of a reasonable excuse for saying no when I'd just offered to do anything I could.

"You'll be there?"

She patted my hand, as if I was the one who needed consoling. I took that to mean no. "You have to promise me one thing. Danny Murdock must not, under any circumstances, take Claude's place. No matter what the committee members say. Do you understand?"

15

Hum Harbour Daze's Steering Committee met in the curling club's boardroom. Boardroom was a grandiose description for the cramped, grey paneled room with orange plastic stacking chairs and scarred folding tables inherited from the Junior High that closed a few years back. There was a glassed trophy case with four top-heavy trophies and a single piece of art on the wall—a framed 1950's print of Her Majesty the Queen. Four venetian-blind covered windows faced the parking lot. When the meetings got boring, you could watch kids skateboarding across the cracked pavement.

The committee normally included Carrie Hunter, (chairperson)—who was glaringly absent—Ross Murray, (committee treasurer), and Vi Murray, (Hum Harbour Daze publicity secretary and Ross's second ex-wife.) Vi and Ross came to verbal blows at least once every meeting.

Reverend Innes was our events coordinator. My oldest brother, Sam, was in charge of fireworks and lobster boat races. And there was me. I represented the Downtown Business Association, and until tonight, I was in charge of nothing.

We sat around the long table sipping take-out coffee while Vi read the minutes of our last meeting and Ross read his treasurer's report. I had a hard time focusing. My mind kept drifting towards my unwanted assignment: ensuring the choice of a new parade marshal went smoothly.

After Ross and Vi, Reverend Innes, resplendent in his rainbow-bright Innes tartan vest, stood and updated us on his progress. Rusty's midway would begin setting up Wednesday. A record forty-three entries were expected in this year's parade; as usual, a local radio personality would be parade judge. Buddy's Dilemma, a popular Celtic rock band, was confirmed for the dance that followed the crowning of the festival queen. Sixty-seven vendors had purchased table-space at the farmers' market/craft sale.

Reverend Innes tugged his vest. "There's a slight complication with the venue, however."

Only half listening, I stared out the window. A man I didn't recognize strolled across the parking lot. Normally, I wouldn't have registered his existence, but these weren't normal days. Claude Oui was dead. Before the man climbed into the pickup parked by the dumpster, he whipped off his cap to rub his forehead. His hair was blue-black—like mine. Apart from his hair, though, he was perhaps the most un-noteworthy person I'd ever noted. I turned back to the meeting.

"We can't use the curling club for the craft sale like we've always done." Reverend Innes rocked up and down on his toes.

Vi continued tapping on her laptop. "Where will it be, then?"

"I'm checking into other options," Reverend Innes said, "but time's running out. If anyone has any suggestions?"

We all stared at the table, afraid if we made eye contact we might inherit the job.

He heaved a weighty sigh and sat.

Sam reported on the lobster boat races: how many registrants they had so far, how many heats required to name a winner, the details of the trophy ceremony—which included a piper, speeches by several politicians, and trophy presentation by Wee Claude, our beloved Highland Heavyweight Champion.

Which brought us to the issue Carrie'd asked me to oversee. Selecting a new parade marshal.

"So who's gonna do it now?" asked Sam. "'Cause if I've gotta ask the mayor or old Bill MacSween, our member of Parliament, I'm gonna have to get on it right away. And then there's the programs. I'm thanking my lucky stars I never got into town to get them printed because I'd just have to do it again on account of what happened."

"Tragedy." Reverend Inness straightened his vest as he stood. "Such a tragedy. Tomorrow is Claude's memorial service, but perhaps we could honor him with a minute of silence during the festival's opening ceremony?"

Vi sniffled.

Ross leaned forward. "Sure, Reverend, but right now we've got a more pressing concern."

Vi gasped. "More pressing? How can you be so callous?" She slapped her forehead with the heel of her hand. "Oh wait, I forgot. Callous is your middle name."

Reverend Innes cleared his throat. "People, please."

Ross ignored him. "Come off it, Vi. It's not like you're any more busted up than the rest of us."

I recoiled at the implication. This might not be the place for tears, but was he actually suggesting we didn't care? That we weren't grieving? If I looked at him, I knew I'd either start calling him callous along with Vi, or start crying. I said to the group at large, "Have we any suggestions as to who might take Claude's place as parade marshal?"

Ross ignored me, too. "I mean, we're all sorry about what's happened. Claude was a fine man, an asset to the community, and we're all going to miss him equally."

That made me feel a little better. Louder, I repeated, "Have we any suggestions as to who might take Claude's place as parade marshal?"

Ross continued, "But this isn't the time or the place to let our emotions get carried away." He finally managed to look sheepish—hard for such a big man.

Following Reverend Innes's example, I stood. "Any suggestions?" I asked for the third time.

"We could invite Bill MacSween," said Sam. "I mean, if the man's coming anyway for our lobster boat races."

"He's done it for the last three years," Ross said. "I thought the whole point of asking Claude was to get away from the political overtones of having our MP presiding over the parade."

Reverend Innes's chair scraped the cement floor when he stood. "Let's not get off track." It scraped again when he sat.

"We wanted Claude because we wanted an athlete. Someone who could appeal to the young people. They're happy to drink at the dance, but they don't care about the rest of the festival."

Reverend Innes frowned, as did I. "I don't think you can make such a generalization," he said. "I know several young people who are happily engaged in the festival. Take our Gailynn, for example."

Still standing, I bowed slightly to acknowledge my status as resident young person. "Does anyone else have a suggestion for parade marshal?"

Ross rested his folded arms on his ample girth. "Well, if we're looking for a local athlete with a good name, then I think we need to consider Danny-Boy Murdock."

"I don't think that's a good idea."

Ross swiveled in his chair. "Why?"

"Because," I said, "It would hurt Carrie. She'd think we thought Danny-Boy could replace her husband. And she specifically asked that it not be Danny-Boy. To go against her wishes would be too cruel."

"Carrie's got to get over that accident, especially now that Claude's gone."

"How can you say that?" I asked.

Vi looked up from her laptop, her eyes misty. "We're not suggesting Danny-Boy could fill Claude's shoes. When you love someone and then you lose them—"

Ross muttered, "Good grief."

"—there's no one who can replace them."

Ross glared at his ex-wife. "How would you know about loving and losing?"

Vi burst into tears.

I rifled through my purse and pulled out enough tissues for both of us. We blew our noses in unison.

"If Bill MacSween and Danny-Boy Murdock are both unacceptable," I said, trying to get the meeting back on track, "have we any other suggestions? Could we make the festival queen our parade marshal?"

Reverend Innes hooked his thumbs in the arm holes of his vest. "Maybe we don't need a parade marshal this year."

"Hum Harbour Daze has always had a parade marshal."

On and on it went, Ross's words growing harsher by the minute. It made me wonder if his gout was acting up, because there was no excuse for that kind of insensitivity. And as the former queen of full-steam-ahead insensitivity, I should know.

Order became impossible. Ross and Vi faced off with another argument.

Sam pounded the table. "Why not Danny-Boy?"

Reverend Innes wrung his hands. "People, please."

The curling club manager stuck his head in to see what all the ruckus was about. One look and he withdrew.

Finally I climbed on my chair and shouted, "I call this meeting to a close! I'll email each of you. You can propose names for parade marshal and email them back to me! Whoever gets the most nominations wins! Thank you!"

Is a meeting considered a success when the women cry?

16

I escaped to the beach. It was dark, and the moon on the waves made the water look like liquid mercury. I sat hugging my knees to my chest and asked God why people were so heartless. I now understood why Carrie felt ill equipped to handle the discussion—or should I call it argument?—about who could replace Claude. I wished I'd run for cover when I saw Carrie sitting outside the police station, because I wasn't equipped for this. I felt like someone had dragged my insides across gravel.

I picked up a handful of beach pebbles, rubbing my thumb over the sea-tumbled stones, and found a piece of glass among them. I held it up to the moon. It was violet, like the earrings I wore. Closing my fingers around the sea glass, I rested my forehead against my knees.

"Are you OK?" It was Geoff. He knew I found solace in the sound of the sea.

"That was probably the most horrific meeting I have ever had the pleasure to be part of."

He sat, and slid his arm across my shoulders. "What happened?"

"People argued."

"And that bothered you."

I leaned my head against him. "Just because I like to argue doesn't mean I enjoy it when others do it." I felt his lips brush my hair.

"I don't see why she asked me to do this in the first place. She had to know I couldn't handle it."

"Any bones broken?"

"No. But it reduced two of us to tears. Three, if you count Reverend Innes."

"Do you think Carrie needs you to stop by?"

I whipped my head up. "Now?"

"She'll be waiting to hear what happened." His hand was cool against my cheek.

I closed my eyes. "I know, but how can I tell her there's no place for the craft tables and farmers' market to set up, Ross Murray's an insensitive jerk, and we made no decision about Claude?"

He kissed me. I noticed he didn't disagree about Ross.

"Do you think if I just called her instead of going to the house? I could make it sound better if she wasn't watching my face."

"What would you want if you were Carrie?"

I let my head hang. "Company."

"I could go with you," he offered. "If she still has lights on, we'll knock at the door, and if the house lights are out, we'll come home again."

That sounded like a tolerable compromise, so I agreed. We walked down the shore until we reached Hunter Hall. It was, unfortunately, ablaze with lights, and we could see Carrie at the kitchen table with my brother, Andrew, and Inspector LeClerc.

"Do you think they have Claude's autopsy results already?" I asked.

"If they do, it's not a good sign."

"Maybe we should leave."

Geoff looked down at me with surprise. "Don't you want to know what they're telling her?"

I was being uncharacteristically uncurious. I knew that. But I had a feeling that if the news was bad, and I was there to hear it, I'd end up spending another night keeping Carrie company. And, all churned up as I was, I was in no shape to offer the comfort she'd need. Besides, I still had the meeting's aftermath to deal with, like emailing the committee members, and tabulating their votes, and—

"Let's go around front and knock on the door," Geoff said.

I followed obediently, across the expansive lawn and around the house. I hooked my fingers through one of Geoff's belt loops so I didn't get lost in the dark along the house's windowless side, on our way to the front door.

Geoff rang the bell, but instead of Carrie, Andrew answered the electronic peal and welcomed us inside. "Man, am I glad to see you." He led the way to the kitchen.

Caber, who was lying on the mat by the sink, lifted his head.

There was a low, pink and mauve floral arrangement on the table. Any other time I'd have found it cheerful, mauve being my favorite color, but tonight its lavender scent screamed funeral.

Inspector LeClerc set a chair for me next to Carrie. Geoff brought another from the dining room.

We surrounded the antique table, no one wanting to be first to speak.

I'd come to offer Carrie comfort, I reminded myself, and touched her arm. "Are you OK?"

She stiffened under my hand but didn't pull away. "I don't think OK will ever be possible again. But I'm alive. That's something."

"Why are you here?" I asked my brother. "You have news?"

Inspector LeClerc answered. "We hoped Madame Oui might remember more about the night her husband died."

"I'm not sure," she said.

"Is there any chance you heard a noise, a scuffle, Claude calling out?"

At the mention of his master's name, Caber waddled over to Carrie's chair. Maybe he expected Claude to join us.

She ignored the dog and twirled her necklace. "Ever since his head injury—I hate calling it an accident because I don't think it was an accident—he's struggled. He doesn't sleep well. Didn't sleep well. So he'd be up making noise at all hours. He tried to be quiet but, well, big men like Claude don't do quiet well."

We waited for her to say more.

"So I guess I stopped listening. That makes me such a terrible person."

LeClerc assured her it did not.

"He could be volatile, sometimes. It was hard to live with."

"Volatile?" Geoff could barely whisper. "Was he abusive?"

"Claude?" She laughed. "Claude was so gentle he refused to own a fly swatter. He'd carry moths outside."

"Then what do you mean, 'volatile'?" LeClerc asked.

"It was part of his Post Concussion Syndrome. One minute he'd be excited, eager, wanting us to move to Africa and change the world, but the next he'd...he'd..." Carrie shook her head, and Caber, apparently giving up on gaining her attention, wriggled closer to me.

I rubbed his velvety ear.

"Claude was a strong man," she continued. "A proud man. I can't talk about him this way. He would've been so humiliated if people realized he wasn't always strong."

LeClerc said, "You're saying your husband experienced episodes of weakness."

Geoff explained. "Symptoms of Post Concussion Syndrome—which Claude suffered—run the gamut, but insomnia, memory issues, mood swings, and depression are common."

LeClerc frowned. "Your husband suffered these?"

Carrie nodded. "It was hard, sometimes, never being sure. One minute he'd be studying Ewe for his trip to Ghana."

Ewe, Geoff once told me, was one of Ghana's numerous tribal languages.

"The next he could barely remember what day it was. And when he was down, he'd lock himself in his office to holler and pray."

Andrew scribbled in his little book.

"Holler and pray," LeClerc repeated. "At the same time, or separately?" Clearly he'd decided Claude was a fruitcake. The way Carrie was painting Claude's recent behavior, I wasn't sure she'd disagree.

"I didn't interrupt, so I don't know."

I decided to get them back on topic. "So the night before you found Claude, he was typically restless?"

"Yes."

Andrew flipped back pages in his book. "Previously, you said you went to bed and to sleep as soon as you got home from your meeting."

"Yes." She sounded a little unsure. "I could see as soon as I walked in the door that he was agitated."

LeClerc nodded, evidently pleased with the additional information. "You'd describe his mood as agitated?"

She wavered visibly. "That sounds too aggressive, too out-of-control. Claude was never either of those."

LeClerc said, "Except when he hollered and prayed."

"He didn't consider that was out of control."

"The night before he died, did your husband tell you why he was—what word would you prefer to use to describe his mood?"

"Unsettled, maybe?"

"Did he tell you why he was unsettled? Or say anything that might have suggested a reason to you?"

Geoff asked, "Did he tell you about Danny-Boy Murdock?"

"No. I already told you that. But…" She got that faraway look, as though she was peering back in time. "He wouldn't look at me. He kept his face turned away. I didn't think anything about it at the time, but if Danny'd hit him, as you said, maybe he was hiding a black eye, or a cut, so I wouldn't get upset. Because I would have been upset if I'd known Danny forced his way into our home."

"He didn't force his way, Carrie. Claude invited him in," Geoff said.

Her red-rimmed eyes widened. "Invited him in?"

"Claude had forgiven Murdock. You know he could never hold a grudge."

She shook her head. "I always told him his kind of Christianity would be the death of him."

This was my first inkling—though I can't say it surprised me—that Carrie didn't share Claude's spiritual awakening. At least not to the same degree. He'd often attended church alone, while she spent Sundays with her mom. I'd assumed the women attended the nursing home's service. But you know what they say about making assumptions.

On my one side, Caber nuzzled my hand.

On the other, Geoff shuffled his feet. "Claude's faith and his willingness to forgive made him a stronger man, not a weaker one."

Carrie's gaze turned challenging. "It made him a poorer man, too."

Considering her graciously-appointed kitchen, with its three-hundred year old antiques and high-end appliances, poorer was obviously a relative term.

I said, "If there's nothing else, maybe we should leave, and let Carrie have some peace and quiet." Everyone, except LeClerc, pushed their chairs back from the table.

"There is one thing," he said.

"And that would be, Inspector?"

"We still await the coroner's report with your husband's cause of death. There is no evidence to connect it with the theft of your frogs, but it seems unlikely the two are unconnected. You should be aware."

Did that mean the police suspected Josh?

Carrie's touch startled me. "Gailynn, do you think…would you mind staying with me again tonight?"

I hesitated—not because I was opposed to staying, but because I still felt ill-prepared to discuss the Steering Committee meeting in a reasonable, calm manner. And she'd ask about it as soon as the men left. "Are you sure?"

"Last night I couldn't sleep a wink. Caber kept howling for Claude. It was terrible."

"I don't think I can do much for Caber."

"Of course you can. The night you were here he didn't make a peep."

The basset bed-hog stared up at me. I found his mournful eyes even harder to resist than Carrie's. "I don't have my overnight bag."

Geoff gave my hand a quick, reassuring squeeze. "I'll scoot home and get your stuff."

"And feed Sheba, please?" By now, my cat would be clawing the cupboards.

Geoff kissed my forehead, and followed Andrew and LeClerc to the front door. As he and Andrew stepped outside, LeClerc turned.

"Your husband was a famous man, Madame Oui and, as to be expected, the press are making inquiries. We have been very careful to discourage speculations, but I cannot guarantee we have succeeded. So when they arrive at tomorrow's memorial service, I would advise you to refrain from making any statement."

Carrie's eyes filled with tears. "Trust me, Inspector, I'll be in no shape to say anything to anyone."

She started up the stairs. "If you could let Caber out for a minute and lock the house? I'm going to take a sleeping pill. I need a good night if I'm to survive tomorrow." She pulled a tissue from her pants pocket and blew her nose loudly before she disappeared upstairs, leaving me alone in the hallway where, three days before, her husband had died.

17

When I whistled, Caber came flying from the backyard, ears out like airplane wings.

I locked the French door, closed the curtain, and turned out the kitchen lights. Then I sat on the stairs. He rested his droopy chin on my knee and gazed at me balefully.

The house was full of shadows. They reached out from the kitchen, the parlor, the great room, crept down the staircase. If it weren't for the brave pools of light cast by the hall lamps, we would have been swallowed in darkness. Of course, I could have flipped on all the downstairs lights, but Carrie's movements upstairs dispelled a good dose of the house's inherent creepiness; and Caber, bless his homely face, was a comfort, too.

"Well, Lord," I said to the other One keeping me company. "Here we are again. Now what do I do?"

A frog figurine stood on the hall table. I could see, from a collector's point of view, it would be an intriguing piece. Unlike Ash's collection, Carrie's embraced a wider frog-aesthetic, although maybe that was because she had more money with which to indulge her obsession.

Thanks to Josh's thefts, Ash possessed who knew how many cheap kitchen frogs. Surely, if he'd really burgled Hunter Hall, he would have presented Ash with Carrie's high-end pieces. Unless he knew Carrie's frogs could link him to Claude's death. After all, Inspector LeClerc did say it was unlikely the two crimes were unconnected.

What would Josh do with the frogs he took, if he took them? Hide them until the heat was off? Chuck them? And how many frogs were we talking about?

Why hadn't I paid more attention when I printed off the insurance claim information?

I pushed Caber's chin off my knee, and headed into the kitchen. Maybe Carrie'd made a second copy of the list. I was unsuccessfully poking through kitchen drawers, when Caber announced Geoff's return.

Geoff had my overnight bag in his hand and a distressed frown on his face. "You left the front door unlocked. Anyone could have walked in here."

"I forgot."

"Forgot? You're the one who keeps saying there's a murderer in Hum Harbour. How could you just forget?"

"Maybe that's how the murderer got in and out without being noticed. Maybe Claude and Carrie never locked their door."

"They always locked up. They have a business in their home, like you do."

"Then I guess I was distracted. Tonight…" I wasn't sure what I wanted to say.

"It's been a hard one." His hug mitigated the reprimand in his words. "Andrew shared some disturbing information after we left."

"What did he say?"

"Until the post mortem report's complete, they can't afford to jump to conclusions."

"But…."

"Livor mortis, that's the discoloration that

happens when blood pools after a person dies, doesn't support the theory that Claude slipped on the loose staircase runner on his way out that morning."

"Oh."

"On top of that, the contusions on Claude's head don't match with what they'd expect if he banged his head." He stood. "Or if he'd simply collapsed at the bottom of the stairs."

"You still think he just collapsed?"

"It's possible he suffered a cerebral hemorrhage after Murdock clocked him. Bleeds aren't always immediately apparent."

I tried not to look annoyed. Geoff wasn't responsible. Why couldn't he get that through his thick head?

"But, according to Andrew, the prelim suggests Claude's head injury was more in keeping with impact against an irregular surface. Like the frog candlestick Andrew bagged. They're checking it for hair and blood of course, but he's doubtful they'll find any."

"So Danny-Boy's punch didn't kill Claude?"

"It may have contributed, but, no, unless he came back later and hit Claude with the candlestick—"

"And took Carrie's frogs so it would look like a robbery gone wrong."

"It's all speculation, Gai, until they find proof."

"Surely the candlestick will have trace— I mean, would the murderer take the time to scrub and disinfect it, knowing Carrie's upstairs?"

"Probably not. But there's another problem with the candlestick theory."

I couldn't guess what.

"Police only found one. Presumably, the other one's with the missing frogs."

I swallowed hard. We were back where I started. The only person we knew of who stole frogs was Josh Pry.

18

The stairs' carpet had been re-secured with a new rod. Despite the woven runner, the stairs creaked beneath my weary feet, apparently rousing Carrie. She called my name in a sleepy voice.

It had been an emotionally draining day; I prayed she didn't have a new list of jobs for me. I tapped on her bedroom door and pushed it open enough to poke my head in. "Are you OK?"

From the depths of her room she said, "Almost asleep, but I wanted to thank you for handling the Steering Committee tonight."

"Yes, about that." Since the situation was unresolved, I'd done nothing to deserve her thanks, much as I appreciated the unexpected words.

"I can sleep easy knowing they didn't choose Danny Murdock. That's all I care about. Can you wake me by ten?"

"Ten?" I was supposed to open the clinic at nine.

"I don't know how late I'll sleep otherwise. Never taken sleeping pills before. And could you vacuum downstairs and dust?"

I knew I'd offered to help, but vacuum and dust Carrie's house when I should be at work?

"Mimi's catering the reception after Claude's memorial service, so you won't need to do any of that work. But people will come here from the church, and I want the place to be presentable. You understand."

Traditionally, our church ladies catered funeral receptions in the church hall. It was their gift to the grieving family, their way of making a difficult time a little less complicated. I guess I shouldn't have been surprised Carrie'd made other arrangements. Carrie was a Hunter after all, and Hunters didn't settle for egg salad sandwiches and oat cakes in the church basement.

Well, Geoff had given me permission to miss work if she needed me. As it was, the clinic would only be open in the morning. Everyone in town would be at Claude's memorial service in the afternoon.

So I said I could handle things. She needn't worry. "Anything else?"

"If there is, I can't stay awake long enough to remember."

"Then, goodnight, Carrie."

She didn't answer. Maybe she was already asleep.

Arching my aching shoulders, I let myself into her office, flipped on the desk lamp, and booted up her computer. The screen saver was a picture of her and Claude. He wore his kilt—only his kilt—and she an elegant, narrow black gown, and her necklace, of course. They made a handsome couple, the tanned, muscle-bound athlete, and his willowy blonde wife.

I found the Steering Committee's address list and sent a brief email to each member, saying they could suggest whoever they wanted, and the one who got the most nominations would be the person we approached first. Hopefully this would work. With less than two weeks until Hum Harbour Daze, we couldn't afford to be fussy about our voting process.

Before I logged out, I noticed a file titled INSLIST on her desktop. I pondered it for a moment then clicked it open. It was an insurance document listing the items missing and their insured value. I didn't take the time to read it—wasn't sure I cared. But in case I changed my mind later, when I wasn't so weary, I printed off a copy and went to bed.

****

Morning came too soon. I'd slept better than the last time I'd stayed the night, but I wouldn't have described my sleep as refreshing. Not that it mattered. Once dawn slanted its yellow fingers through my open window, I pushed back the covers and attacked my duties. I walked Caber along the shore—finding three pieces of lime-green glass—made myself breakfast, called Geoff, hunted down Carrie's cleaning equipment, dusted, vacuumed, straightened, took phone messages—all-around Girl Friday stuff.

At ten, I presented Carrie with a breakfast tray: a dish of fresh fruit, toasted bagel smothered with cream cheese, and a mug of strong coffee. She looked like a Scarlett O'Hara sitting in her massive bed surrounded by plumped pillows. All she needed was that spectacular bed jacket.

There was something weird about Carrie, I thought as I left her alone. The way her emotions flipped on and off. Sometimes she seemed truly devastated, and other times…other times it was like she almost enjoyed the attention. As if it was her due.

I shook my head as I stepped into the shower. Grief was too big an emotion for me. I would never understand it. I would never understand capricious Carrie—capricious being a word my mom often used to describe me, though I don't consider myself unpredictable.

With each hour, I seemed to be getting sucked deeper and deeper into Carrie's life. Any personal plans I might have had for the day—like work, Dunmaglass, Hum Harbour Daze planning—I set aside. After my shower I helped Mimi set up for the post-memorial reception, arranging stacks of dainty luncheon plates and folded napkins, clearing spaces for floral arrangements, ensuring the Hunters' tea service was ready for use. In other words, I polished the silver.

With no time left for lunch, I hurried home to change. I allowed myself about sixty seconds in Dunmaglass. I wanted to be sure Ash was ready for a possible influx of customers before and after Claude's memorial service—which was mercenary, I knew, but necessary nonetheless.

Then I drove Carrie's SUV into Antigonish to pick up her mother. I knew, even before I accompanied Geoff while he visited patients in the poshy seniors' residence where Phyllis Hunter lived, that Carrie's mom had very exacting standards.

So I set a fresh box of tissues on the console between the front seats, adjusted the AC until the car's inside thermometer read a comfortable twenty-two degrees Celsius, and selected a classical music CD from Carrie's collection. I prayed my efforts would earn me a modicum of civility.

Phyllis Hunter waited in a wheelchair in the mirrored foyer of the Inverness Arms Seniors' Residence. She wore a veiled black hat and oversized black mink stole. I was warm in my sleeveless black dress.

I greeted Mrs. Hunter and her caregiver.

"She sent you?" Mrs. Hunter grabbed a strand of

my hair when I leaned close. "I told her I didn't want the black one."

So I should color my hair? I gently disentangled it from her knurled, arthritic fingers. "I'm sorry you feel that way, Mrs. Hunter. But I promised your daughter I'd help her as much as I could. This afternoon's going to be hard for her."

"Do you think I don't know that? I've lost my husband, too, you know."

"I'm sorry," I said automatically.

"Don't patronize me, girl. I know you don't care a hoot about my loss." She glanced back at the caregiver pushing her chair towards the waiting car. "Hurry up, and get me into that ridiculous contraption, or I'll be late. If I make it there at all. I told her I didn't trust this one's driving."

I was sure Mrs. Hunter knew absolutely nothing about how I drove.

The caregiver gave me an apologetic smile as she assisted Mrs. Hunter into the SUV. I climbed in the driver's side and double-checked the seatbelt was properly attached—Carrie'd warned me her mother worried about buckles not holding.

Mrs. Hunter rapped my fingers with her brass-handled cane. "Don't touch me, girl! I have enough strangers pawing me. Every day there's someone new in this infernal place. Just get used to one nurse, and they replace her with another."

"I'm sorry."

"Is that all you can say? I'm sorry? I assumed your mother would teach her only daughter to speak up for herself, instead of mincing. I'm sorry. I'm trying to help." She puckered her mouth when she mimicked me.

I bit back a reply and pulled out of the parking lot. Blessed silence lasted less than a minute.

"You trying to get us killed, too? Open your eyes, girl." She pointed at the car stopped at the red light. It patiently awaited its turn to go through the intersection while I proceeded. I had the green arrow. I was supposed to proceed.

"There've been enough deaths around here. We don't need any more."

I kept my mouth shut.

"Do you think we need more deaths?"

"No, ma'am."

She exhaled a blast of air from her nostrils. "I suppose you're another one of his fans?" I noticed she never used people's names.

"You aren't?"

"A grown man who tosses telephone poles? Maybe if he'd put in an honest day's work now and again."

"Your son-in-law was a champion athlete."

"Is that what you call it?"

"Carrie's very proud of his accomplishments."

Mrs. Hunter grunted. "Over-sized biceps don't make a man."

"I don't mean to disagree, but Claude Oui was much more than that. He was honest, and kind, and he loved the Lord."

She sniffed derisively. "He loved the Lord a darn sight more than he loved his family."

I thought that was supposed to be a good thing.

"Honor your parents. That's what the Good Book says. But he was running off to Africa, wanting my daughter to go with him. And leave me here alone."

I almost said I was sorry again. "There are lots of

folks at the Inverness Arms. You wouldn't be alone."

"Don't contradict me, girl."

"I'm sorry."

She stared at me until I felt my cheeks growing warm. "I suppose you're one of those born-again types like he was?"

I flashed a sideways glance trying to gage her intent. "I'm a Christian."

"And you think I'm not?"

I kept my sights glued on the road ahead, although our conversation had turned more dangerous than the winding pavement. "I have no idea, Mrs. Hunter. Do you love the Lord?"

She blew air from her nose. "Trust a MacDonald to think that's all that matters in life."

"I'm sorry?" I bit my lip. I shouldn't have said that.

"Head in the clouds, the bunch of you. Not a whiff of common sense. And you, about to marry that missionary."

"Geoff's a doctor."

"I know he's a doctor. Don't I see him every time he comes by the home? And you trailing along behind like some smitten little puppy."

"Panther cub," I said.

"I beg your pardon?"

"Geoff says I remind him of a young panther. Black hair." I gave it a tug for emphasis. "Brown eyes."

Behind her veil, her eyes narrowed.

I couldn't resist one last panther trait. "Hunts at night."

"The man lives dangerously," she said. I thought I detected the first hint of civility, perhaps even respect, in her tone.

19

I parked in front of the church and accompanied Phyllis Hunter to the heavy wooden doors propped open for the occasion. Across the street a white CBC van, replete with its characteristic red logo, stood with the side panel open and a camera running. I could hear the journalist discussing our congregation's Trinitarian roots. Like most people who've speculated over the years, she was wrong.

Third Church was called Third because First Church burned down in 1875, and its replacement, Second Church, went the same way in 1922. Third Church, it was hoped, would survive longer, and so far, it had.

I escorted Mrs. Hunter to the choir room—which doubled as the church parlor—where Carrie waited with Reverend Innes.

"Mom!" Carrie sprang from the worn plaid sofa, and engulfed her mother in a hug. "Gailynn found you all right?"

"Of course she did." Mrs. Hunter patted Carrie's back. "The girl's lived here all her life. She'd hardly get lost."

I hid my smile. "If that's everything, I'll leave you two with Reverend Innes."

Geoff would be somewhere in the congregation, holding a seat for me.

Carrie caught my wrist. "There is something,

actually, Gailynn, if you don't mind."

Annoyance bubbled inside me before I could squelch it. "If it won't take too long. Geoff's waiting."

"I was wondering if you might forgo the service and scoot back to my house to help Mimi with the reception preparations."

"I think everything's well in hand."

"I know, but I'd feel so much better if Mimi had an extra set of hands in case something unexpected came up."

"Carrie." Her name was all I dared to say. I mean there was help—the kind I'd already offered—and then there was help—the kind she now demanded. Frankly, she was becoming tyrannical.

Be charitable, I told myself, she has no one else to call on. "Let me talk to Geoff. I don't want to leave him alone if he needs me."

She nodded curtly.

There were a lot of people in the sanctuary I didn't recognize.

Geoff assured me he'd be fine. Would I? He squeezed my hand—he could tell my patience was growing thin—and promised to join me at Hunter Hall as soon as the service was over.

I left Carrie's SUV for her and her mother and walked the few blocks down to Hunter Hall. It had turned into a dreary day, the kind where tumbling clouds blocked the sun, and the cooler August wind blew from the east. Goosebumps spread across my bare arms and I kicked off my shoes and walked faster. Cars parked along every street filled Hum Harbour to the brim. People in funeral clothes eyed me suspiciously as I scurried barefoot in what they surely considered the wrong direction.

So be it. I had a new assignment for the afternoon—caterer's assistant. And though I regretted leaving Geoff, spending the next hour with my cousin Mimi wouldn't be painful. We might look like night and day, well-padded, freckled Mimi with her curly, auburn hair, and straight haired, curve-free me, but we loved each other, and we loved the Lord. Two people couldn't get more alike than that.

I'm not sure how best to describe the rest of the day. I could go into excruciating details about the menu Mimi'd prepared, the number of pots of coffee consumed, who came, who didn't, what they wore, what they said to Carrie, and what they said behind her back—a lot of colorful comments about Carrie's frogs. Claude's trophies, strategically placed around the downstairs, received almost as many mentions. I washed teacups, fetched boxes of tissue, restocked bathrooms, emptied trash, and kept Caber from getting underfoot. I welcomed people. I bade them farewell. I couldn't tell whether Claude's family came or not. Who knows, maybe that black-haired fellow I first saw in the curling club's parking lot, whom I today found wandering around upstairs looking for a bathroom, was a relative.

When it was all done, when the last guest had left, and Carrie'd taken her mother back to Antigonish, I helped Mimi clean up. Geoff helped, too. We returned the house to its pre-reception condition, or as close as we could remember, so that when Carrie finally reappeared, all she had to do was lock the door and go to bed.

Geoff agreed to take Caber home with him, since Carrie insisted she'd never sleep with the dog prowling and howling all night.

It was almost ten. The fog had rolled in. The old-fashioned cast iron street lamps the town had installed along Main Street glowed eerily, giving Hum Harbour the flavor of Sherlock Holmes's London.

I wore Geoff's suit jacket over my sleeveless dress. My shoes dangled from one hand—my feet too weary to stuff back into the strappy heels.

Geoff had unfastened his top shirt buttons, his tie hung loose, and his white shirt was stained and wrinkled.

Caber plodded forlornly between us.

Every now and then a vehicle drove by, and we could hear, but not see, a gang of kids carrying on the way teenagers do.

We'd walked maybe half a block when a man climbed out of a car parked beside the curb. He stood in the middle of the sidewalk, blocking our path.

Already spooked by the swirling fog, I shrank deeper into Geoff's jacket.

20

The man wasn't especially tall, but he was built solid as a cement wall. I'm sure it would've taken two hand-holding adults to encircle his girth. I didn't need to see his face to recognize Danny-Boy Murdock.

"I wanna talk to you," he said.

"About what?" Geoff sounded as unnerved as I felt.

Danny-Boy clicked his heels, drawing my attention to his signature, tasseled loafers. He was known to wear them with everything from his kilt to his shorts. Presently he wore a rumpled suit. "I can't very well approach Carrie myself," he said.

I silently agreed. That would not have gone well.

Geoff said, "I'm not sure what that has to do with us."

"He was my friend."

Danny-Boy looked so miserable, standing there with his head hanging down.

"I'm sorry Carrie's so hard on you," I said.

"I don't blame her. I haven't exactly behaved like a friend." He stepped closer, his slurring words floating on a cloud of whiskey fumes. "And the last time I saw Claude I was a horse's fanny."

"Is that what you wanted to tell us?" Geoff asked.

"I wanna talk to Gailynn, here, and ask her to talk to Carrie for me."

"And say what?" I asked incredulously.

"That I'm sorry. That I never meant to hurt Claude—neither time. I know we argued and kibitzed around, but we were friends. She's gotta believe that."

"I don't think she does," I said.

Danny-Boy's massive shoulders drooped. "She's got you believing I'm a criminal, too?"

"I have no idea if you're a criminal. Maybe you are, maybe you aren't. But I'm not going to be able to convince her one way or the other. That's up to you."

"How am I gonna do it when she won't even talk to me?"

I shook my head. I had no idea.

"If I was parade marshal, maybe then she'd see I'm only trying to help."

Geoff gave Caber's leash a sharp tug. He'd been about to water Danny-Boy's shoe.

"Bad idea." Geoff could have been talking to Danny-Boy or the dog.

"Why not? I know Carrie's gonna stew over who'll take Claude's place as parade marshal. Other women might forget about something like that, but not our Carrie. She's conscientious to the nth degree, and we all know Hum Harbour Daze is her baby."

"You taking Claude's place would be disastrous."

"Listen, I know I can't replace him, not in any true sense, but I could fill in for him. I know how important it was for Claude to support Carrie's projects. That man loved his wife."

"I'm afraid the committee's already nominating Claude's replacement. It's just a matter of hearing whether or not that person accepts."

Technically that was true. Once I went home and tabulated the votes and asked whoever came out on top whether they'd accept the position, it was just a matter of waiting for their answer.

"I see," said Danny-Boy. "In that case, I guess I'll head home." Danny-Boy lived a good hour away.

Geoff placed a restraining hand on his arm. "You're not driving are you?"

"I don't see why not."

"You've been drinking—"

"One," he said defensively. Whether he meant one drink or one bottle was up for debate.

"The police'll be out in full force," Geoff said. "I have a futon. You could sleep there."

Danny-Boy brushed away his hand, and his offer. "I'm good. Really. I'll just take my time. Cops won't even notice me."

There wasn't much else we could do, short of calling the police ourselves, so we let him go. Geoff walked me the rest of the way home and he and Caber bid me goodnight at my door. I didn't invite them in. Sheba would eat Caber. Not that she's a nasty cat. It's just that Caber was so plump and droopy and irresistibly mild mannered, he wouldn't stand a chance against my twenty-three pound huntress.

I locked myself and my cat in for the night, made a pot of Mimi's herb tea, lit a few candles, and treated my cold, weary bones to a bubble bath. I left checking my emails and the entire Hum Harbour Daze parade marshal issue for the morning.

****

Basset howls can raise the dead.

At least they raised me from a dead sleep.

Despite my bath, it had taken a good hour to squelch thoughts of Claude's memorial, Claude's widow, and Claude's rival, but I'd finally fallen asleep. And now, thanks to Claude's dog, I was awake again. I hugged my pillow over my head, but it had little effect. I could still hear Caber's forlorn, hair-raising howls. With two pillows crammed over my head, I could barely breathe, but Caber's howls still came through loud and clear. Why wasn't Geoff quieting the wretched animal?

I kicked off my bed covers. Pulling my oversized hoodie over my pajamas as I let myself out onto my deck, I didn't stop to consider what I planned to do about the noise. Probably stomp across the bridge and bang on Geoff's door until he smothered the dog.

Not really.

But what I found—once my eyes were opened and focused—silenced me.

Geoff sat on the deck, back against the building's stone wall. Caber huddled between his legs, howling his little heart out, while Geoff rubbed his ears. It wasn't calming him, of course. And sitting there with his eyes closed and the dog's deafening howls ringing in his ears, he wasn't aware that I was there watching tears run down his stubbled cheeks.

I hesitated, not sure whether to sneak away and let them grieve in private or offer comfort neither probably wanted.

Without opening his eyes Geoff said, "It's OK."

"I'm sorry."

He held out his hand, and I hurried to accept it. I plunked down beside him, my head against his shoulder, and cradled his hand in both of mine. Acknowledging my presence, Caber rested his chin on Geoff's thigh, finally quiet.

"I guess it's a good thing you're my only

neighbor," Geoff said. Downtown Hum Harbour, with its drafty old stone buildings overlooking the wharf, was not prime residential territory.

"I see why Carrie can't sleep once he gets started."

Geoff caressed Caber's long ear. "Didn't he howl when you were there?"

"He snored and hogged the bed. Does that count?"

"I guess he likes you."

"Or, maybe he only howls with folks he's comfortable with."

A quiet chuckle shook Geoff's shoulders. "Aren't I lucky?"

I could see the red rims of Caber's eyes as he gazed up at Geoff. Grief and hope, as though he half-expected Geoff to transform into his beloved master. Wouldn't that have been a great trick? An instant answer to all his sorrows.

"I called the cops," Geoff said. "I thought about it when we came in. About Murdock driving home in the fog after drinking who knows how much. I did nothing for Claude, and look how that ended up."

Danny-Boy would not appreciate Geoff's concern, we both knew that, but I was glad Geoff had made the call. "Did you hear anything back?"

"No. And I don't expect to."

Silence. I didn't know what time it was. No moon or stars. No ripples from the shifting tide. No pre-dawn birds. Not even a car engine in the distance.

It was over a year since Geoff had returned from Somalia, and, for the most part, he'd easily slipped back into Hum Harbour's quiet routines. But there were times when his experiences returned to haunt him. Sometimes he let me join him. As if by holding my hand, he could keep the most unpleasant memories at bay. When he was quiet, like he was now, I knew he was losing the battle.

I patted Caber's head, suddenly wishing he'd fill the vacuum with another mournful howl. Bring Geoff back to the present. He didn't. Instead, Caber angled his head until he could lick between my fingers. I pulled away from his tickling tongue.

Geoff pressed his lips against my hair. "You don't have to stay with me. I'll be OK."

I knew he would. Geoff's belief in God's gracious plan had survived tests I couldn't begin to grasp and his faith had come out stronger, more unshakable than mine would ever be. That was a big part of what had attracted me to Geoff in the first place. His good looks made him seem unattainable, but his wounded heart, his unflagging belief that God could heal it, and his willingness to trust me with his pain, made him irresistible. I loved Geoff before I ever recognized it. And the depth and fierceness of that love sometimes startled me.

"Tell me about Claude," I said. Perhaps sharing his memories might help.

"You don't want to hear all that."

I snuggled against his side, making myself comfortable. "Sure I do. I want to hear about every moment you can remember."

He could remember a lot. I'd not realized how close Geoff and Claude had become. Men like my father and brothers tended to maintain their men-friendships on a camaraderie kind of level—shared work, shared antics. They didn't discuss their dreams, goals, hurts, or theology—at least not that I was aware of. But Geoff and Claude did. Geoff was a mentor to Claude. He taught Claude how to pray, confess, and discern God's voice. He taught him to obey God's lead and expect God's healing.

"Claude had a falling out with his family before he met Carrie. And he never told her about them. Or them about her, for that matter. The two parts of his life were completely separate. Like the Christian part and the athletic part."

Caber's back leg twitched, and Geoff stilled it with the gentle weight of his hand.

"The idea that God wants to be part of our whole life, not just our Sunday mornings, excited Claude. And I think it frightened him, too, though he never admitted that." Geoff smiled. "You should have seen the way he squirmed before he told Highland Breweries he wanted out of their endorsement contract. I made up an errand so he wouldn't be alone on the trip to Halifax. But I knew he was fretting by the way he kept pulling at his shirt front. He did that whenever he was nervous. You could tell, before any competition, how confident he felt by how much he adjusted his shirt."

"Did everyone know that?"

"Anyone with two eyes would pick it up soon enough. Murdock used it against him, until I told Claude he was telegraphing his tension to the other competitors." He shook his head. "I should have kept my mouth shut."

"If it gave the others an unfair advantage over Claude…"

"Well, Highland Breweries didn't need to know Claude was nervous about cancelling his endorsement. We prayed before he went into the meeting, and when he came out, he climbed into the car and sat there grinning like a hyena with a water buffalo. 'You were right,' he said. 'I told them the endorsement conflicted with my new commitment to God, and I had to follow my conscience. I even quoted that passage—you know the one where Peter says, 'You yourselves judge what is right in God's sight—to obey you or to obey God.' And, what could they say?'"

"We'll sue?" I suggested.

Geoff chuckled under his breath. "Yep. That was it. But he was so happy. So proud of standing up for what he believed, that they could have drained him of every penny he'd ever earned, and he would have thanked them for the opportunity to stand firm."

I pictured Claude's face and the way it shone whenever he had a chance to talk about Jesus and forgiveness and his new life in Christ. I'd never seen anyone so luminous. I knew that was a strange word to describe a person's face, but I suspected it's what the Old Testament Israelis thought about Moses whenever he stepped out of the tabernacle tent, his face glowing so bright they begged him to cover up.

Geoff's back deck faced east. The first glow of dawn crept above the watery horizon, lightening the indigo sky. Morning birds celebrated the coming sunrise with song.

Geoff stretched, and I sensed a subtle shift in his mood, as well as his body. The initial ripping of loss had passed. His friend was gone, but Geoff could still remember Claude's faith. And with each remembering, with each telling, the celebration of Claude's faith would grow.

Geoff was healing. Again.

He made me go home to bed, to catch an hour or two of sleep before I had to begin the day.

A little stiff, a lot weary, I did as he suggested. But

in the back of my mind I was once again thinking about Claude's other legacies: his grieving wife, his closest rival, and the silly Hum Harbour Daze parade, which threatened to bring the two face to face.

21

My morning, which arrived within the hour, was promised to my mother. After I checked my emails and informed everyone that the nomination process was inconclusive, I showered, dressed, and headed home for breakfast. I love living above Dunmaglass, but the house I grew up in would always be home.

Mom was up to her elbows in soapy water, cleaning the dishes from Dad's breakfast. It might be Saturday, but as usual, he was off fishing by sunrise. She glanced over her shoulder, greeting me with a smile.

"You're early."

"Am I?" The old wall clock said seven-thirty. Like everything else about my mom's kitchen, it had been there as long as I could remember. "I couldn't sleep, so I figured I might as well get up."

"I assumed you'd be exhausted after Claude's memorial service."

"And helping Carrie," I added, in case she'd forgotten. "I am exhausted, so please, where's the coffee?"

"I intended to put on a fresh pot. Can you wait that long, or do you want instant?"

Instant was good enough. I plugged in the kettle and ladled coffee crystals into a mug still hot from the sink.

"I have a problem that needs your wisdom," I said

as the kettle slowly warmed. "You've had lots of experiences with schoolyard feuds."

Mom was, after all, a retired teacher.

"It's been a while, but I suppose, like most things, it's a skill that comes back to you." She stripped off her rubber gloves. "Who's feuding now?"

"It hasn't exactly happened yet. I'm hoping you can help me preempt the battle."

She plunked the cast iron skillet on the stove, turned on the element, and added six strips of bacon. Soon they were sizzling cheerfully.

"Carrie asked me to chair the Hum Harbour Daze Committee's last meeting, which didn't go well. We have to pick a replacement for Claude for the parade marshal, and no one could agree, so I sorta made an executive decision. We'd each nominate someone, and whoever got the most nominations would be parade marshal—assuming they agreed to it when I asked them."

She forked the bacon to the edge of the skillet, and added two eggs. "No one came out ahead?"

I stared impatiently at the kettle, desperate for just enough boiled water to make my coffee. "Everyone nominated the same person."

"Then what's the problem?"

"They nominated Danny-Boy Murdock, the one person Carrie will refuse to accept."

My mother nodded sagely.

"I don't get it. I mean, I know she thinks he clobbered Claude on purpose that one time, but even if it was intentional, nothing was ever proved. He was never charged. And like it or not, in most people's eyes, he's Claude's successor. Who can blame the other committee members for nominating him?"

Mom poked the egg yolks with a fork and flipped them, flooding the kitchen with mouthwatering aroma. I took a plate from the draining rack, and held it while she transferred my breakfast from the pan to the plate. Still no whistle from the kettle.

"Is there something else going on that I don't know about?"

Mom joined me at the table. "Nothing that time shouldn't have healed long ago."

My fork stalled half way to my mouth.

"There was a time when Dan Murdock paid favor to Carrie Hunter."

I gaped.

"Their parents were friends—the Hunters and the Murdocks—and they endorsed the union."

"You make it sound like a business merger."

"I'm sure that's not how they saw it. Still, they sent Carrie to St. FX"—Saint Francis Xavier University in Antigonish—"no doubt hoping she'd be thrown into social events with young Dan. He was a good looking boy, promising student, star of the football team. They probably hoped nature would run its course, and by graduation they'd have the son-in-law of their choice."

"Except she met Claude Oui."

"Hmmm. He came from Cheticamp."

Cheticamp was a small fishing village on Cape Breton.

"Oldest in a large family. Poor, like most fishing families in those days." Mom chewed the inside of her cheek. "We were lucky. I had a good teaching job, so the lean times were never too lean for you kids. But the Ouis had eleven mouths to feed. A university education was out of reach. Besides, I'm sure Claude's father needed his help fishing."

My oldest brother, Sam, fished with our father, allowing Andrew the luxury of entering the police force, and me—well, women do fish, but my terror of water ruled it out as a career path. I guess that's partly why I became a medical receptionist on dry land.

"Claude was bright, determined. He earned enough scholarships to pay his way. If I'm not mistaken, he ended up with a degree in Commerce."

"And Carrie."

"And her, too." Mom smiled.

"And her folks?"

"Not impressed with the French boy from Cheticamp. But they loved Carrie to distraction, and if Claude was her choice, they were prepared to accept him."

"How did Dan Murdock feel?"

"You know, I was never sure Dan would have fallen in with their parents' plan in the long run. And to be honest, from my point of view, Carrie made the better choice."

Mom loved Claude. She'd often comment how, when he accompanied Carrie to the Inverness Arms where her Mom lived, he'd leave the women chatting, and visit other folks—the ones who had no one. He'd listen to their stories, never talking about himself or his accomplishments. He'd hold a hand, or give a hug.

"Where was Claude's family during his memorial service?"

"I wondered that, myself" said Mom. "Maybe they didn't appreciate Claude leaving home."

"But to carry a grudge that long?"

"Feelings run deep, Gai." Mom patted my hand, and changed the subject. "That nice Inspector came for supper last night."

I assumed she meant Inspector LeClerc. "Shouldn't he have been investigating Claude's memorial?"

"He had to eat. " She chuckled. "But he asked me the strangest thing—at least I thought it was strange in light of that ridiculous conversation we had the other day—about someone stealing kitchen frogs."

"It wasn't ridiculous."

"That's my point. Raoul— "

"Who's Raoul?"

"Raoul LeClerc. He seems to think there's some merit to your theory."

"You see." I savored the last bite of egg.

"Andrew, of course, likes to play the Devil's Advocate."

"I told him he needs to talk to Ash."

"About her frogs?"

"And her boyfriend. Josh has been pinching kitchen frogs for her. She wants to return yours, by the way."

"I should say!"

I dragged a piece of toast across my plate, soaking up the last traces of egg yolk, and popped it into my mouth. "It doesn't help me decide what to do about the parade marshal thing."

"What does Geoff say?"

"Claude was his friend."

"He feels caught in the middle?"

"I think so. I haven't asked." I pushed away my plate. "I wish I could just push Hum Harbour Daze back a month, and give everyone a chance to grieve. Maybe, by then, the decision would be easier."

The kettle finally reached a boil, and mom poured hot water into my mug. "How do you think Carrie will react if you choose Dan Murdock?"

"She'll go ballistic. And I don't want to be anywhere near her when she does."

"Do the committee members know who they each nominated?"

"They might, depending on how much they talk to each other."

"So you couldn't announce that your own candidate won?"

"I don't have a candidate."

"You could come up with one."

"What good would that do? My one vote against all the others?"

She sighed. She did that whenever she was growing exasperated with me. "Does the parade need a parade marshal?"

"It has always had one." In Hum Harbour, always was reason enough for anything.

"Have you prayed about it?"

I squirmed. A panicked help counted, didn't it?

Mom rested her elbows on the table, and her chin on her cupped hands. "When do you have to decide by?"

I copied her stance. "Soon."

"Then talk it through with Geoff. He's wise. He'll have a good sense of what Claude would have wanted to happen."

I felt the weight lift from my shoulders. "What Claude would want. That's a great way to frame it for Carrie." I scooted around the table, and hugged my mother. "You're brilliant. I knew you'd know what to do."

She looked a little bemused, but she hugged me back. "If that's settled, can we talk about bridesmaid dresses?"

"I thought we'd already found one we liked."

She carried my dishes to the sink before I had a chance to grab them. "That was just the beginning. Now we have to draft patterns, choose colors, find fabrics—"

In other words, a shopping trip to Antigonish. Not what I had in mind for the rest of my day.

22

"Did you get a chance to stop by the jeweler?" Geoff asked that evening. He was leaning over my shoulder, reading the email I'd prepared for all Hum Harbour Daze Steering Committee members outlining our dilemma. I couldn't put it off any longer.

I shifted my laptop and patted the couch beside me. Sheba sprang from the floor, to the coffee table, to the vacant spot on the couch.

"You know what shopping with Mom is like. Every possible sale has to be checked just in case there's something for the wedding. It's getting way out of hand."

"Then tell her."

"I try. Not that it does any good."

"Do you want me to talk to her?" Geoff settled beside me, relocating Sheba to his lap.

"It'll be OK."

"You just said—"

I leaned against his shoulder. "The truth is, as long as she keeps things the right color, I'll survive. Besides, I can probably talk her out of a lot of the extravagances given the time frame we're working with."

"Unlike your committee."

"What am I going to do? I have to get this parade marshal business settled."

"I think that's a good start." Geoff read my email aloud. "The committee members have unanimously nominated Danny-Boy Murdock to replace Claude Oui as parade marshal. In light of our committee chair Carrie Hunter's previously expressed concerns, I am personally uncertain how to proceed. I fear that contacting Mr. Murdock will ignite a confrontation. Things will be said, feelings hurt, bridges burned—perhaps never to be rebuilt. I am not convinced this needs to happen. Is there nothing we, as a committee, can do to head this off before it's too late?"

"Does it sound too unprofessional?"

"It sounds like you care. Isn't that the message you're trying to get across?"

"Yes."

"Then send it, and see what kind of response you get."

Sucking in a deep breath, I said, "We haven't got a lot of time to haggle over this. The parade's in"—I glanced at the calendar on the wall—"six days. And we still need to publicize the change."

"I wouldn't worry about the publicity angle. Word will pass like wildfire as soon as you've decided."

"Especially if it's Danny-Boy Murdock."

He scratched between Sheba's ears, and her purr hiked up a few decibels.

"I can't help wondering if there's more between Danny-Boy and Carrie than Claude's head injury. Though, I suppose, when the person you love's been hurt…" I shook my head. "You and Claude were close. What do you think?"

"They've been rivals for years, but it's been mostly friendly."

"Mostly?"

"Guys, testosterone, and beer are an aggressive mix."

"I thought Claude quit drinking."

Sheba rotated her head so Geoff could scratch under her chin.

"He did. But Claude's sobriety made Murdock uncomfortable. And the money Claude made off of the Highland Ale endorsement—well, Murdock didn't hide his opinions. He accused Claude of hypocrisy."

My computer chirped. The first return email popped into my inbox.

"And Claude agreed with Murdock. The Highland Ale contract contradicted his new life. For a while, he rationalized it by setting the money aside to pay for his upcoming mission trip."

Dissatisfied with only one person's attention, Sheba pulled my hand close. Automatically, I petted her.

"What did Carrie think of that?"

"He never came right out and said, but I think it caused problems. Hunter Monuments and Toys is in survival mode. It doesn't do much more than put food on their table. Losing the endorsement income was significant."

A second message notification chirped. Sheba rolled onto her back.

"So Carrie blames Danny-Boy for Claude's head injury and losing the Highland Brewery's money?"

"It's probable." He shifted to see my face.

"Last night, when Danny-Boy stopped us on the street and offered to fill in as Claude's replacement, do you think he was being genuinely kind or maneuvering his way closer to the Highland Brewery endorsement?" I shied away from introducing my mom's theory that Danny-Boy might harbor lingering feelings for Carrie.

"The beer endorsement? That's a pretty cynical suggestion."

"Am I wrong?"

"I don't know him well enough to know what really motivates him. Greed? I suppose it's possible. And remorse, and grief."

"He was Claude's closest rival. I mean, with Claude gone, Danny-Boy's number one."

"Only in Canada. He has a long way to go to become the International Champion."

"But, if you add the fact he punched Claude the night he died, it starts to look pretty incriminating. Don't you think?"

The third message alert sounded. Sheba responded by exposing her belly.

"I don't see how we can ask Danny-Boy to be parade marshal."

"See what the others say."

"What if they don't care about Carrie's feelings?"

"No one is that heartless, Gai. They were just looking for the easy way out of an awkward situation, and choosing Murdock as parade marshal probably looked like a quick fix."

"You think?"

"Open them up and see."

I checked the messages.

I suggested Danny-Boy Murdock as parade marshal because he approached me outside Claude's memorial service and offered himself. He wanted to make things a little easier for Carrie. He seemed sincere. But you're right. Danny-Boy sitting in Claude's seat will only make it harder for Carrie. I'm sorry. I should not have let Danny-Boy's tears sway me.—Vi Murray

It's too late to keep haggling about this. If you don't

want our opinions then why did you ask? Have no parade marshal. It makes no difference to me.—Sam

Murdock approached me. He said he'd already talked to the other committee members. I assumed Murdock being the new parade marshal was a done deal.—Ross Murray

Reverend Innes's was the last message to pop up. Geoff squeezed my hand, and I opened the final email.

Grief is a complicated emotion, and perhaps we've been wrong to accept the seemingly simple solution Danny-Boy Murdock offered. In light of Gailynn's email, leaving the position vacant might be the wisest option at this point. It honors Claude's memory among us, and it respects Carrie's wishes.—Reverend Innes

Geoff and I silently reread Reverend Innes's email.

"Who has the authority to make the final decision?" he asked.

I thought back over Carrie's original dictum, her sitting in the car outside of the police station, dabbing her eyes and blowing her nose and asking me to chair the discussion. "Me, I think."

"Then what do you want to do?"

I snapped the laptop closed and set it on the coffee table. Sheba rolled over and eyed me suspiciously. "What do you think?"

"I think I'd like to know what you want to do."

I could hear Ash downstairs. Apparently she was talking to someone—probably Josh—and I strained to hear what she was saying. It was a good way to avoid answering Geoff.

Until he poked me in the ribs.

"What I want is for this whole thing to go away. I want to have never told Mimi I'd take her place on the Steering Committee. I want Claude to be alive, and Josh to give back all those stolen frogs, and Carrie—I want Carrie Hunter to go back to ignoring me."

Geoff pinched the bridge of his nose.

"But, since none of those are going to happen, I guess I'll have to settle for calling Carrie and telling her we are going without a parade marshal this year because Claude is irreplaceable."

Geoff let go of his nose.

"Does that sound reasonable to you?"

He kissed me. "Infinitely."

Feeling warm, wise, and content—a pleasant side effect of Geoff's kisses—I dialed Carrie's number. It rang through to her machine. She could have been screening her callers. She could have been asleep. She could have been crying out in her garden. I debated whether to leave a message outlining the committee's decision—well, my decision. I settled for, "Call me when you get this."

I guess she didn't get it for a while.

****

Sundays were routine. I didn't see that as a negative thing. Predictability was comforting. I knew what to expect. With me ignoring the complications of Carrie and Hum Harbour Daze, that Sunday started out like any other.

First: church, which most folks avoided in summer, even if they were home. I personally enjoyed the informality of our summer services, when Reverend Innes forgot his clerical gown and showed off his tartan vests, instead. Summer worship music changed too, as our organist and choir stepped aside, allowing different members of the congregation to share their musical gifts. My favorite Sundays were the ones when the MacKay family brought their fiddles. This wasn't one of those Sundays, however. Today we had off-tune, bluegrass worship with a backdrop of fading funeral bouquets left over from Claude's memorial service.

Reverend Innes's sermon was about finding God's grace in the midst of grief, and in a strange way, the music and flowers fit the message. I wasn't surprised that Carrie didn't attend.

Following service there was the usual post-service coffee time—well, iced tea time—on the church lawn. Geoff and I stood to the side, Geoff's hand on my waist as I fielded the reverend's questions about the Hum Harbour Daze parade marshal. I kept my voice down and explained I'd yet to talk with Carrie about the final decision. But I was following his advice. I would recommend we leave the parade marshal position vacant this year. Until Carrie Hunter concurred, however, I didn't want the news made public. I promised as soon as Carrie gave her OK, I'd notify Vi Murray, and Vi could notify the local papers and radio station.

Mid-afternoon, we MacDonalds began congregating at my parents' house for the weekly family dinner. During the winter, it was roast beef and mashed potatoes. In summer, it was BBQ ribs and potato salad. You'd think as a family of fisherman, we would favor seafood at all family gatherings. But the truth was we avoided it.

Dad said it went back to the days when kids like him were the poorest of the poor. Taking seafood lunches to school—not peanut butter or bologna like the other kids—made them a laughingstock. I guessed he'd never outgrown that feeling. So Sundays we ate beef.

We filled the yard with people and webbed lawn chairs. Because Hum Harbour was built on a hillside, backyards sloped precariously. Unless one added a deck onto one's house—which my folks hadn't—tipping lawn chairs were part of every summer gathering. Over the years, we'd each marked out a spot where our chair wobbled the least.

Geoff was a welcome part of the family gatherings long before we became engaged.

He was Sam's brother-in-law and Andrew's best friend. So, besides my parents, Andrew, Geoff, and me, there were Sam, Sasha, and my new niece. Sam and Sasha adopted three-year-old Mara at Easter. She was absolutely adorable, and the main attraction at any gathering. There were also Ash's family—her parents, brother, sisters—and Josh, of course. And cousin Mimi, her husband, Mike, and their two boys. That made nineteen of us. Usually there were more, but two other families were away at a softball tournament, and another aunt and uncle had decided to go RVing every weekend in August.

The afternoon progressed in the usual fashion, hardly worth mentioning, except for a brief conversation I overheard—quite by accident—between Andrew and Geoff. They were standing under the apple tree at the bottom of the yard, gazing toward the harbor, and I thought, considering the direction they were staring and the way they were pointing, that whatever they were talking about had something to do with the water. Which had nothing to do with me.

Until I caught the words "head injury." The only important head injury I knew anything about was Claude Oui's so I inched closer and listened.

23

"LeClerc's shown me the preliminary report," said Andrew. "I've gotta tell you, it has me concerned."

"What's the problem?" asked Geoff.

"For you—great news. No way Murdock's punch had anything to do with Claude's death. His T.O.D., time of death, has been set between midnight and one. You were both long gone by then. Right?"

Geoff nodded.

"We're working on the theory Claude surprised a burglar."

"Carrie's missing collectables?" Geoff asked.

"LeClerc had me contact the Ouis insurance broker. Who would think those frog doo-hickeys of hers were worth more than a buck-a-dozen at the dollar store?"

"They're valuable?"

"A small fortune."

I watched Ash and Josh chase Mara between the lawn chairs.

Andrew continued. "We're trying to trace them. Can't be many frog collectors out there. Most likely scenario, whoever took Carrie's frogs will try and dump them at pawn shops or sell them online."

"What if they just hang onto them until the heat's off?"

"Always a possibility. But we're going with the theory our thief wasn't the brightest amphibian in the pond." Andrew chortled when he said amphibian. "He'll likely make another mistake that'll help us identify him."

I had two questions. He? As in Josh? They'd focused on him? And what did Andrew mean, another mistake? OK, that was four questions. Of course, I couldn't ask any questions of my own without alerting Geoff and Andrew that I'd been eavesdropping.

As though sensing my thoughts, Josh slowly turned. Our gazes met, held, and I was the first to look away. My stomach ached with concern. If the frog thief murdered Claude…

Somehow, I had to get into Ash's room and search her frog collection. I had a copy of Carrie's list, the one I'd downloaded the night I slept over. If I took it with me and checked Ash's frogs against the list and confirmed she didn't have any, it would go a long way toward proving she and Josh weren't involved. Wouldn't it?

But what if I found something of Carrie's hidden amongst Ash's things? What would I do then? Tell Andrew? Convince Ash to tell him? Would she betray Josh? Or would she cover for him, even if it meant he was a murderer?

Twenty feet away, they stood with heads together, whispering. If only I could read lips.

I was so consumed with my thoughts and so oblivious to everything else, I didn't hear Geoff come up behind me. I jumped when he slid his arm around my waist.

He grinned, ignoring Andrew's quip, which I had also missed. "Where were you just now?"

"Lost in space."

He kissed the tip of my nose. "Well come on back

or you're going to miss dessert. Mimi brought cheesecake."

"Only one?" One cake would never feed all of us.

"You're right. She must have brought two. Let's check the kitchen."

We found three cakes in the fridge. Geoff and I sampled one and took our plates to the front step where we could sit and talk uninterrupted. He let me get a forkful of rich, creamy cake into my mouth before he asked, "What were you thinking about, really?"

I took my time swallowing. "When?"

"Out back when I startled you. You were staring at Ash and Josh."

My cheeks warmed with guilt. "If you must know, I was trying to decide how I could get into Ash's bedroom."

"And what?"

"See if she had any of Carrie Hunter's missing frogs."

"Do you really think that's possible?"

I poked my fork into the raspberry swirls in my cake. The very thought of Josh's guilt almost killed my appetite. "I hope not."

"But, you can't stop wondering?"

"Am I wrong to wonder? To be afraid she might be involved?"

"Josh's already stolen frogs for her. True, they're only kitchen frogs, but maybe, like Andrew and the rest of us, he didn't realize Carrie's collection was worth so much." He poked at his cake, apparently suffering the same malaise I had. "He thought they were trinkets."

I nodded. "How could he know they were anything more than cheap, ceramic figurines?"

"But we can't break into your uncle's house to check our theory."

"It wouldn't be breaking in. They never lock their doors, and I'm always welcome, any time. So are you."

"Not once they realized what we've done."

"What do you suggest? Wait until Andrew turns up with a search warrant? That would be even worse." I could tell, by the tensing muscles in his jaw, Geoff agreed.

"Everyone will be hanging around here for another hour, at least. What if we say we're going for a walk, and we'll be back in a little while?"

"What if someone wants to come along?"

"My family? Walk?" My family considered exercise to be grueling work and never attempted it on a Sunday. "We'll have to be quick. I've a copy of Carrie's insurance list at home. Can we get that, check Ash's stuff, and be back here in an hour?"

"We'll have to."

I scraped the last streaks of cheesecake off my plate and licked the fork. I guess I hadn't lost my appetite after all. "You tell Dad we're going for a walk, and I'll stick our plates in the dishwasher. Meet back here in five minutes."

****

Ash's room was full of frogs. I mean *full*. She made Carrie Hunter's collection look like the dabbling of an amateur. Stuffed toys. Posters. Sketches. Dresser-top containers. Books and bookends. Even her wallpaper. Frogs everywhere. But were any Carrie Hunter's?

I went first. Geoff hovered in Ash's open bedroom door, apparently uncertain whether to risk entering.

Doofus, the family dog, had no such hesitation. He pushed past Geoff, jumped on her bed, and promptly fell asleep.

Under Ash's bed, I found plastic containers. I dragged them out and pried off the lids. Inside them we discovered enough Kermits to sink the navy. Frog slippers in sizes she'd outgrown. Frog-faced tea plates wrapped in bubble wrap. When Ash was eleven, she bought them with the money she'd been saving to get her ears pierced. If only we'd known where Ash's frog obsession would lead.

Doofus rolled onto his back, his tongue lolling out of his mouth, and started snoring.

I felt immensely relieved we'd found nothing incriminating. We re-stowed the plastic containers under the bed, snapped off the light, shut the door, and hustled back to my parents' house.

Just in time, too. Everyone was gathering their kids and empty dishes to head home for the evening. Had we been five minutes longer, Ash's parents would have caught us in their house.

That's when I remembered Doofus was locked in Ash's bedroom where he was never allowed.

24

I tried to intercept Ash. She and Josh always left at a more leisurely pace than her parents. Maybe they would've moved faster if Ash realized I'd left Doofus shedding allergens all over her room.

Andrew leaned against his pickup, looking as if he had nothing more pressing than a burp on his agenda. But I recognized the keen light in his eyes, and I watched him watching them. Something was up.

Freeing Doofus would have to wait.

"Hey, buddy," he chin waved to Josh. "Gotta minute?"

Josh straightened. Did he sense danger? Tugging Geoff's hand, I maneuvered us within hearing distance.

Andrew said, "Gotta question for you, buddy. A favor to ask."

"A favor?"

"Question. Favor." Andrew shrugged. "Maybe answering my question's the favor."

Josh's brow furrowed as he absorbed that.

"You told LeClerc you followed Murdock from Hunter Hall. Did you go back? Later."

Josh slid his index finger under his do-rag, and scratched. "Why would I do that?"

Andrew studied Josh through deceptively casual eyes. "Make sure everything was all right?"

"Well, I guess, yeah, I think I might have, like,

wandered by a little later."

"What time?"

Josh shrugged. He didn't wear a watch. He didn't pack a PDA. How would he know what time it was? "Midnight? Maybe."

No longer looking casual, Andrew leaned forward. "Notice anything?"

"Like some guy watching the house from across the street?"

"Someone was watching Hunter Hall?"

Josh shook his head. "Not that I saw."

"Then why did you say that?"

"Gai asked me if I'd seen anyone. I thought you two were, like, talking about the same guy."

"You saw no one," Andrew repeated for clarification.

"Except Danny-Boy Murdock. He was standing by the door in the dark."

I couldn't keep my mouth shut. "What was he doing there?"

"Ringing the bell? Then Claude invited him in."

"At midnight," Andrew said.

"You're sure?" I asked. "I mean you're sure it was Danny-Boy?"

It was Josh's turn to glare at me. "I'm not, like, stupid. I know the dude when I see him."

"And you saw him go inside Hunter Hall at midnight the night Claude died?" asked Geoff.

"He didn't stay very long."

"You saw Murdock leave? Again?"

Josh, apparently unaware of how potentially incriminating his answers were, nodded. "Maybe five minutes after Claude let him in. I hung around the Hall, on accounta how his first visit ended up. I thought, like, Wee Claude might need me for back up, in case he and Danny-Boy started trading punches again."

"They did not trade punches," said Geoff. "It was one punch by Murdock."

It was also preposterous to imagine Josh backing up Claude in a wind storm, let alone a fight. "Did Wee Claude need you?"

"Na. He was, like, smiling and they shook hands when Danny-Boy left."

"And you went home."

"Well," admitted Josh, "I did hang around a little longer—until all the lights went out."

Andrew slapped Josh on the back the way men do when they're being friendly. Perhaps, he meant to convey satisfaction with Josh's answers. Perhaps he wanted to rattle Josh's composure along with his teeth. Because his next question sure did.

"Is that when you broke into Hunter Hall and stole Carrie Hunter's frog collection?"

Josh's mouth fell open.

Ash's blue eyes blazed with fury. "H-how could you ac-c-cuse Josh?"

Her reaction momentarily silenced Andrew. Or maybe it was the group of curious family members—Mom, Dad, Sam, Sash, Mara, me, and Geoff—gathering behind her that made him stop before this turned into a full-fledged interrogation. Dropping his arm across Josh's narrow shoulders, he pivoted them until their backs were toward us and we couldn't see their faces.

"Yes or no? You can tell me here or at the station," he said to Josh.

"No!" Josh jerked free. He crossed his heart,

scout's style, and we all saw it.

"S-see." Ash fixed my brother with a withering glare. "He's innocent. If you're g-going to treat people like criminals, s-see if we ever come back for Sunday dinner!"

Naturally, Mom had a thing or two to say to Andrew.

****

Geoff and I walked to the rocks beyond the end of the beach and stopped at Hunter Hall as we retraced our steps home.

It was dusk. I couldn't put off talking to Carrie. We scooted around the house to the front door without being seen. An unknown green pickup was parked beside the curb.

Carrie answered the door so quickly that she must have been in the front room, though no lights brightened the windows. She sounded out of breath. Or angry.

I unconsciously stepped back a pace and came up hard against Geoff's chest. "Is this a bad time?"

She pushed her flowing hair out of her eyes. "It's been a long day, Gailynn. Is this important?"

I self-consciously flipped my ponytail over my shoulder, hoping I did not look as intimidated as I felt. "I left several messages for you."

"I'm aware of that. I just wasn't ready to see anyone."

Fair enough. But this couldn't wait. "It's less than a week until Hum Harbour Daze, so I've made an executive decision about the parade marshal."

She hadn't turned on the entrance light. With only

the hall lights behind her, I couldn't make out her expression.

I felt Geoff's hand on my shoulder. "Maybe, Carrie, if you asked us inside, we could sit and talk this through?"

"Is there something that needs talking through? I thought Gailynn said she'd made the decision."

"But in respect to you, and Claude, and your feelings, she is seeking your confirmation before making it public."

Carrie tossed her hair. "Look, Gailynn, if I thought you needed me to hold your hand through this, I would never have asked you to step up. If the job's too hard, say so. I admit this is a painful time for me. But if the Steering Committee needs me, I'll come back. Hum Harbour Daze has been the major local event for nearly a century, and I won't leave it to implode on my watch."

"It's not imploding. And it'll survive perfectly well without a parade marshal. For this year, at least."

Carrie sucked in her breath. "Excuse me?"

"The committee's decided, in honor and respect for your late husband, we will not select an alternate parade marshal. Claude is irreplaceable. And we won't even try."

Carrie fished a tissue from her pocket and wiped her eyes. "The committee decided that?"

With my input. "Yes."

"They really didn't choose Danny?"

Geoff assumed his empathetic, doctor face. "Would that have been so hard for you?"

"Impossible." Her lower lip started to tremble. "That man has been the bane, bane of our lives for so long, that it rips my heart, rips it right out, to imagine him benefitting from my tragedy."

"No one is benefitting from this, Carrie," Geoff said.

She blew her nose into the tissue. "I'd really like to be alone."

She made me feel like an absolute heel. Obviously, she was just trying to hang on to her last shreds of composure, and here I was forcing Hum Harbour Daze concerns down her throat. "I'm sorry, Carrie. I just wanted you to hear the committee's decision from me and not on the radio or something. I didn't mean to bother you. Really. I understand."

I was silent as we walked home. I didn't know what to say. On one hand, I grieved for Carrie. She had no one to share her pain except her mother in the nursing home and the dog she'd pawned off on Geoff. She was, quite literally, alone. I was trying to fill that gap, but between our age difference and our lifestyle differences, we had nothing in common. And apart from ordering me around, she seemed to have no interest in developing a friendship.

Although maybe I was being too hard on her. Who made friends when they were grieving? Not that I wanted to be her friend. She could be very cutting.

"She was the one who came after me, asking me to chair the Steering Committee. I never wanted her job."

Geoff squeezed my hand. "I know."

"I don't even know why she asked me. I mean, I'm the least capable on that committee."

"I don't believe that."

"I just went on it because Mimi begged me to take her place. You want to know something?"

He raised his eyebrows.

"Mimi told me, after I said yes, that she was tired

of dealing with Carrie. Carrie's too bossy. I thought, hey that's fine with me. I didn't want to take on any heavy responsibilities anyway, not with all the stuff Mom's got me doing for our wedding. I thought I'd be a body warming a chair. That's all. Certainly not a body occupying the chair."

Geoff hmmed understandingly.

"And it wasn't like I was trying to back out of it. I told Carrie I'd help as much as I could, and I was helping. I am helping."

"Yes, you are."

"And for her to jump down my throat like that. She did, didn't she? I'm not being oversensitive?"

Geoff drew me into his arms. "Carrie is hurt, and grieving, and she probably doesn't know which way is up right now, but you did not deserve what she spewed at you." He kissed me. "You have been nothing but patience and kindness to her this last week."

I snuggled closer. "I thought you sounded very understanding."

"Thank you."

"And taking Caber is very generous."

"She has him back now."

"Oh. He didn't even come to the door to see you."

Geoff gave a half-laugh. "He's a dog. No one teaches them etiquette."

Reluctantly, we resumed our pace. The scent of August herbs wafted toward us as we passed the kitchen garden beside the Hubris Heron. Geoff took the few pieces of sea glass we'd found on our beach stroll out of his pocket. "Tonight's cache," he said, closing my fingers around them. "Are you ready for our appointment tomorrow?"

"Do you know what kind of ring you want?"

"A plain band that won't harbor bacteria."

"That should simplify your choices."

"Sorry you're not marrying an artist or a millionaire?"

25

Love was a strange thing. Knowing you were unconditionally cared for could be as intoxicating as any drug. Sometimes it calmed your soul, leaving you floating in the inexpressible peace. At other times, it excited. The unlimited possibilities of life pulsed through your mind and stirred your body. You were loved.

My heart hammering with anticipation as I imagined my future with Geoff. I couldn't sleep.

I read for a while. I vacuumed. I scrubbed the bathroom sink. I knelt beside my bed and prayed. In the end, I got dressed and went back to the beach. When all else failed, the rhythm of the sea always soothed me.

Flashlight in hand, I wandered along the shore looking for glass and humming. Humming soothed me, too. I got as far as the end of the beach and the rocks Geoff and I had climbed earlier and turned back. As I passed Hunter Hall, I happened to look up. It was the middle of the night; I expected the house to be in darkness and Carrie sound asleep. That's probably why I hadn't bothered looking when I walked past it the first time.

But the house wasn't dark and Carrie, very definitely, was not asleep.

She and the black haired man I'd caught wandering her house looking for a bathroom stood in her kitchen. They seemed to be arguing. He waved his hands; she stood rigid, arms folded tight across her chest. He reached toward her, and though I was too far away to see for certain, it looked like he grabbed her necklace—the one Claude had given her—and yanked it from her neck. Carrie's hands flew to her throat then she covered her face as though she was crying. After a moment, the man put his arms around her and patted her back.

How should I interpret what I'd just seen? Obviously, Carrie knew Black Hair well enough to allow him into her home. And accept his embrace. Who was he? What were they arguing about? Why did he grab her necklace?

I went home, but I still couldn't sleep.

****

The clinic was closed Mondays. Even though Geoff was Hum Harbour's sole doctor, there really wasn't enough business to keep him going five days a week. So he did things like visit area nursing homes and make the odd house call. Yes. He made house calls. When he was doing those, he didn't need my services. Such was the case that particular Monday morning, and I decided to take advantage of the freedom by doing a little sleuthing on my own.

I didn't tell Geoff what I had in mind. I didn't consult Andrew. I knew what both would say. But seriously, I had no intention of doing anything questionable. Searching Ash's frog collection had convinced me Josh was innocent of burgling Hunter Hall and bludgeoning Claude. Time to turn my attention to another possibility.

I determinedly pushed the scene between Carrie and Black Hair from my mind. I needed to think long and hard about what I'd witnessed and instead opted to investigate Mom's theory. Did Danny-Boy harbor unreciprocated feelings for Carrie Hunter-Oui?

Maybe being torn between three men—her beloved Claude, Black Hair (whom I was not thinking about), and Danny-Boy—explained Carrie's contentious attitude the previous night. The idea sure made me feel contentious, and I wasn't even involved.

After my morning beach walk and before I began sleuthing, I reviewed the receipts for last week's sales at Dunmaglass. As I'd expected, the shop did very well with Claude's funeral patrons.

Sheba made herself comfortable on my lap. For a very large cat she could curl into a very compact ball, and for some unknown reason, she seemed to enjoy it when I rested my laptop on top of her. Maybe she liked the warmth? Anyway, that's what I did. The Internet and the modern preoccupation with sharing useless information had turned everybody's life into an open book. I Googled Danny-Boy Murdock, accessing pages of hits; no matter how boring, I read each one.

Among fan-favorite details like his height, weight, eye color, and marital status, I learned Danny-Boy was thirty-six. He'd attended St. Francis Xavier University in Antigonish on an athletic scholarship during the same time as Carrie and Claude. He didn't complete his degree.

I searched photos from the university's archives, cross referencing Danny-Boy, Carrie, and Claude and found two grainy shots. The first depicted a group of toga-clad students crammed into a very small room—looked like a closet really—with a punctured beer keg.

Froth and liquid spurted from the keg like a geyser. Claude tipped his face heavenward, trying to catch the stream. Most of the others in the closet seemed to be laughing uproariously. Carrie's wet hair and toga clung to her body as she watched Claude with enraptured delight. Danny-Boy watched Carrie.

In the second photo, taken at an X-Men's football game, Claude was once again the central figure, once again surrounded by a laughing crowd, once again the focus of Carrie's rapt attention. Danny-Boy Murdock stood to the side. He wore a mud stained football uniform and a caustic frown.

Most current references and photos of Danny-Boy, the highland heavyweight contender, were of little help. A couple of speculative mentions of Danny-Boy as Wee Claude's successor as Highland Brewery's new spokesman. Nothing definitive. And a few dozen articles referring to the hammer-throwing incident that almost ended Wee Claude's career. They depicted Danny-Boy as sincerely distraught about the accident. One included a snapshot of Claude, this time on a stretcher about to be loaded into an ambulance, tearful Carrie holding his hand, and Danny-Boy watching from the sidelines. Of course, the caption writer credited the anguished expression on Danny-Boy's face as for wounded Claude. I, however, thought distressed Danny-Boy was looking at Carrie—but maybe that was just me. And hardly conclusive.

Looking at a woman, no matter how suggestive your expression, did not make you guilty of jealousy-fuelled homicide.

I logged off and went next door to the Hubris Heron and my cousin Mimi. As owner/manager of Hum Harbour's most popular eating establishment, she was privy to all sorts of gossip. Surely she'd know something—if there was something to know.

Mimi was in the kitchen wearing a turquoise apron emblazoned with a hideous orange lobster. She scooted around the room so fast you'd've thought she had on rollerblades.

First came the mandatory hug, then taste testing the chowder simmering on the stove. Then I was free to plunge into my reason for coming.

"The other day Mom said she thought maybe Danny-Boy Murdock was still carrying a flame for Carrie Hunter."

"Still?" asked Mimi. "You mean he was before?"

"I don't know. That's why I came to you."

She had some kind of herb or spice in her hands. Rubbing it back and forth between her palms, she rained rust-colored flecks into the chowder. She stirred. "Well, I suppose he's always been attentive to her, now that I think about it."

I helped myself to an oatcake. "In what way?"

Mimi returned to the dough she'd been kneading. "I'm remembering her father's funeral. How Danny hovered out of reach but always within earshot. Phyllis, of course, always treated Danny-Boy like a surrogate for his father. You knew she and Big-Dan were an item back in the stone age?"

"I can't believe she's only a couple of years older than Mom."

"A lot of health issues over the years."

I knew that, of course. She'd been Doc Campbell's patient until she'd moved into the Inverness Arms and transferred to an Antigonish doctor.

"So you think it's possible?"

Mimi scooted back to the soup and stirred. "Sure. I

guess. All things are possible."

"But is it likely?"

She fixed me with a penetrating stare. "Why do you want to know?"

"I've been helping Carrie out a bit, and frankly, I feel like I'm getting caught in the middle of something."

"Well, her husband just died."

I made a face. "Besides that. Danny-Boy keeps trying to insert himself into Carrie's life. He says he wants to simplify things for her. Claude was his friend. He wants to honor their friendship by assuming Claude's responsibilities, like becoming Hum Harbour Daze parade marshal. Maybe he means well. But maybe he's trying to take advantage of the situation for his own benefit."

"But you're not sure."

"Geoff's suspicious, but…"

"But?" She waved her hand, encouraging me to finish the sentence.

"Claude wasn't. He welcomed Danny-Boy into his house. He shook his hand. He treated Danny-Boy like…a friend."

"Maybe Danny-Boy was pulling the wool over his eyes, too."

"You think so?"

"I always say go with your gut."

"My gut?" I'd never heard her say that.

"What's your gut telling you?"

I sniffed. The delicious fragrance of seafood chowder, rising bread dough, and fresh baked oatcakes made my stomach grumble. "My gut says I'm hungry."

She laughed. "Grab a bowl, and taste drive the chowder. Enough curry?"

Mimi put curry in chowder? Not the info I'd come looking for, but it was interesting.

****

I'd arranged to meet Geoff at three at Piteaux Jewelers in Antigonish. We were going to pick out his wedding ring. Mine was already purchased—an etched gold band the jeweler had designed to go with my diamond, which had been Geoff's mom's diamond before it was mine.

According to my watch, I had two hours to fill. I decided, since I was on a roll with this Danny-Boy thing, that I might as well head into town early and see what I could find out about Danny-Boy there. I didn't have a specific plan on how.

The sun hung in a cloudless sky. I cranked down all four car windows, and let the wind tangle my hair as I drove along the twisty coastal road. I passed two new house constructions along the way. Cute little bungalows with wide windows and ample yard space. Geoff and I'd never discussed where we were going to live once we were married. Not in his apartment above the Hubris Heron, surely. It suited his non-materialistic sensibilities but, from my point of view, it left a lot to be desired. Nor was my place over Dunmaglass exactly made for family life. That's assuming we planned to start a family straight away. We hadn't talked a lot about that, either.

I rounded a sharp bend, where the mountainside pressed smack up against the road's shoulder on one side and a pond—swamp really—languished on the other. Standing with his back to the rock face, and his thumb in the air, was Josh Pry. Why wasn't he out on the boat with his dad? I slammed on the brakes, shifted into reverse, and backed up until I was beside him.

He rested his hands on the car's roof and poked his head in the open passenger side window. "Hey, Gai, am I glad to see you. Can I bum a ride into town?"

"You're not out fishing?"

"Give me a ride, and I'll, like, tell all."

I invited him to climb in, enjoying a sense of serendipity as he buckled up. Josh liked to skulk around. Maybe he knew something about Danny-Boy.

Bing! Light bulb moment.

What if, on his last night, Claude confronted Danny-Boy about his misplaced interest in Carrie? Claude was a gentle man but, if his relationship with Carrie was threatened, or if he at least thought it was threatened, or, better yet, if Carrie had told Claude about Danny-Boy's unwanted attentions...

I smiled at Josh and locked the car doors before pulling back onto the road.

26

Josh's reason for being stranded at the side of the road? He was on his way to get a part for his dad's boat engine when his car broke down. He couldn't afford a tow, so he'd started to walk. I'd been so lost in thoughts about my future with Geoff, I hadn't even noticed his abandoned vehicle, which is amazing since Josh drove a fire-engine red hearse from the 1960s. No one should ever miss it.

I kept my eyes on the speedometer, making sure I stayed under the speed limit, to prolong the time I had with Josh. "You know the night you saw Danny-Boy at Hunter Hall? Did you happen to overhear anything he and Claude said?"

"I already told your brother I didn't hear nothing."

I flashed him what I hoped was a reassuring smile. "I know Andrew can be kind of intimidating when he's in full cop-mode. When he gets like that with me, I can hardly remember my own name, let alone something I half heard days before. I just thought maybe, now that you've had time for stuff to percolate, you might remember something. Not the exact words, but maybe the gist of a conversation. Or their tone of voice?"

I felt Josh's gaze slide over me, then away. "It's complicated."

"Whatever's said in my car stays in my car." I wasn't sure if that convinced him, or just gave him the needed excuse to vent.

"See, if I did hear something it'd mean I was, like, someplace I was maybe not supposed to be. You know?"

"But could you say what you heard? Or what you saw? When you were where you weren't supposed to be?"

He turned sly. "Anything in it for me?"

"Even if what you told Andrew is true, and you didn't help yourself to Carrie Hunter's frogs, you did steal from other people. Do Ash's parents know about that?" I checked the rear-view mirror. I counted five cars behind me. If I went much slower, I'd start a riot. "So what did you hear?"

"They were, like, 'How did you get them to reconsider?' And, 'Nothing's definite. It's in your camp now.'"

That sounded like they'd been discussing the Highland Brewery's endorsement. "They weren't talking about Carrie?"

"Why would they talk about her?"

I glared at Josh. "Because Claude found out about her and Danny-Boy."

"Carrie and Danny-Boy? That's twisted."

"That's all you've got? Claude and Danny-Boy discussing what? Beer?"

"What did you expect?"

"I don't know. Something incriminating."

A pickup, three cars back, pulled into the oncoming lane, and floored it. As the he drew alongside, another vehicle sped around the curve toward him.

I hit the brake. The guy coming towards us swerved onto the gravel shoulder. The pickup cut in front of me, barely missing my front bumper. The car behind me blasted his horn, and its driver flashed a middle finger salute. I saw it in my rear view mirror.

Josh gripped the dashboard. "Idiot!"

"You OK?"

He pried his fingers from the padded plastic, and slowly eased back in his seat. "No thanks to that idiot."

"Life's full of the unexpected." I sounded much calmer than my white-knuckled hands suggested. "You never know what's coming around the corner."

"Like what happened to Claude? You going to start preaching?"

"Do you need preaching?"

"Nope. I know what you're gonna say, anyway. I've been to church."

"Then you know what you've been doing is wrong."

"No one cares about kitchen frogs."

"Ash does. Isn't that why you've been stealing them for her?"

"So?"

I held up my left hand so he could see my engagement ring. "See that? It belonged to Geoff's Mom. It's second hand, so it didn't cost him anything to buy it. The value of this gift isn't about how much it cost. The value is in the love it represents. Stealing second hand kitchen frogs and giving them to your girlfriend, doesn't say love. It says you don't care one bit about her. It says you're cheap and inconsiderate and untrustworthy."

His face folded into a scowl.

"Are you cheap and inconsiderate and untrustworthy?"

He stared out his window.

"Is that what you want Ash to think about you?"

"No."

"Then do the right thing. Give back the frogs. Tell Andrew what you saw and overheard the night Claude died. Be the kind of man Ash always thought you were."

****

I parked on Main Street, and fed nickels into the meter, my mind still on the conversation with Josh. Maybe he'd take what I said to heart, and do the right thing. Or maybe he wouldn't. Either way, it sounded like my theory that Danny-Boy carried a torch for Carrie Hunter needed a little more verification before I could claim it had any relevance in Claude's untimely death.

I had no idea where I'd find that verification.

Why had I decided to walk south along the shore past Hunter Hall the morning Claude died? If I'd gone the other way, I never would have heard Carrie scream. I never would have run into her house, never would have offered to help, or agreed to chair that stupid Steering Committee meeting. Instead I'd be happily planning my wedding and hypothesizing about missing kitchen frogs. I would be totally unaware that Ash's boyfriend was a thief. That Hunter Hall groaned during thunder storms. That Caber Oui desperately loved his master, or that Danny-Boy harbored inappropriate feelings for another man's wife. Like David, Bathsheba, and poor Uriah. And look where that led.

No, if I'd simply walked the other way, I wouldn't be caught in this web of mistrust and doubt. I wouldn't be reading hidden meaning into fifteen-year-old photos. And I wouldn't be imagining that someone I knew was a killer.

I'd been here before and, despite what Geoff said about murder making my eyes shine, I did not like it. I liked quiet. I liked uneventful. I liked normal.

Or was I just lying to myself?

27

I spent the next hour perusing the archives at the local newspaper. I was looking for anything sensational or incriminating about Danny-Boy. The Casket's archives only went back a few years, so there was nothing about his university career. Archived photos focused on his recent athletic activities as a highland heavyweight contender. There were, of course, several articles about the Wee Claude incident, but they didn't tell me anything I hadn't already read on the Internet. And one small article, a four-liner tucked on the bottom of a page thirteen, commented on a court appearance for drunk driving charges. That was five years ago.

Nothing about his social life, though. Nothing to suggest a penchant for murder.

Disappointed, I gave up my search. It was time to meet Geoff and pick out his wedding ring. That, at least, lifted my spirits.

****

The buzzer sounded softly as Geoff and I entered Piteaux Jewelers. A waist-high display counter ran the length of one wall, a floor to ceiling showcase along the opposite. The carpeted space between was narrower than a grocer's aisle. Piteaux's was a family run business, and our Mr. Piteaux, busily setting maroon-velvet ring trays on the glass-topped counter, was a third generation jeweler. We were a little late for our appointment which, apparently, was not a problem. Or maybe he was just glad we'd finally made it after three cancellations.

"Your men's wedding bands are quite varied these days." Mr. Piteaux's voice had an abrasive nasal tone, as if his sinuses and adenoids were perpetually inflamed. It always made me wince.

"You have your yellow gold band, your white gold, and your platinum. There's your plain, your etched, and your embellished. If there's a style you favor, but you're not taken with the metal or gem stone, we can always customize."

Geoff nodded, his gaze focused on the trays of rings.

"The wedding's next May, am I right? That gives us lots of time." Mr. Piteaux smiled at both of us although, as I said, Geoff was too busy staring at all the rings to notice. "Do you have any specific preferences or requirements? Are you wanting to match Gailynn's ring? These days your young couples like their matched sets."

"No," said Geoff, unable to drag his gaze from the selection. "I need something plain and durable."

Mr. Piteaux pushed his specs up his nose. "Excellent. An excellent start. Color preference?"

Geoff shook his head. "I have no idea. Should it be the same as Gai's?"

"If that's what you want. Why not try one on, see what you both think." Mr. Piteaux picked out a gold band and, taking Geoff's hand, slid the ring onto Geoff's third finger.

It looked awful. Geoff's skin was perpetually

tanned—the result of his time in Africa—and in summer, he tanned even darker. The yellow gold made his hand look jaundiced.

Geoff glanced at me, and we both shook our heads. Not yellow gold.

"Excellent," agreed Mr. Piteaux. "Let's try the white."

Better, but all the rings Geoff tried looked incongruent with his long-fingered hands.

That left the platinum rings which, frankly, were beyond our predetermined price range. Well, my predetermined price range, since I was the one paying for Geoff's ring. But, considering my recent conversation with Josh, I wasn't about to scrimp. I watched Geoff model the platinum rings, holding out his hand, this way and that for the three of us to see.

That's what we were doing when the electronic buzzer hummed, and the shop door swept open.

Black Hair—whom I'd been intentionally trying not to think about—stepped in with a whoosh of hot air, took one look at me standing there with my mouth hanging open, and whooshed out.

I could've been wrong, of course. I mean, maybe he'd entered the jewelry store by mistake. Maybe, he wanted personal time with Mr. Piteaux and didn't appreciate sharing the jeweler's attention.

I stepped closer to Geoff, and safety. Neither he nor Mr. Piteaux seemed to find Black Hair's hasty exit concerning. But they didn't know what I knew about him.

"What do you think of this one?" Geoff asked.

He wore a piece of pipe on his finger. That's what it looked like—a centimeter-wide slice of unpolished pipe. A piece of copper plumbing would have looked more elegant. And yet, it was perfect. The width, the simplicity, the overwhelming masculinity. I could tell by the way he stretched and fisted his fingers, that he liked it, too.

"I think that's the one," I said.

"Excellent," said Mr. Piteaux.

Geoff slid the ring back onto the tray, and I fished in my purse for my credit card. For the first time in my life, I was about to bump my limit.

28

We drove home in separate cars, Geoff first, me following. With my brain in semi-automatic mode, I paid more attention to my thoughts than the road.

What had Black Hair wanted at Piteaux's? When we left, I hadn't noticed him lurking nearby, waiting to see Mr. Piteaux in private. Would he go back to the jeweler's now that we were gone? Why was he avoiding us? Because it sure felt like he was avoiding us. Had he seen me that night, standing on the beach in the dark? Surely not. Maybe he remembered me from the reception at Carrie's. But why would that disturb him?

Thoughts of Carrie led to thoughts of Steering Committees, parade marshals, and Danny-Boy. Although the committee had no real obligation to tell Danny-Boy their decision about the parade marshal, he needed to be told. I thought I'd volunteer Ross Murray for the task. Ross was heavy-set and well respected—two qualities Danny-Boy understood.

But there were other issues I needed to deal with.

I needed to think through my conversation with Josh and figure out whether I should wait for him, or tell Andrew that Josh might be holding out on some important information. In a strange way, I felt a need to protect Josh. Why? If the kid was breaking into houses and stealing stuff, it was only a matter of time until he started doing worse. Maybe he was already doing worse.

"Lord," I said aloud, "we need some time together for You to sort my thoughts. When I get home, could we have an hour, just You and me, some place quiet?"

Hum Harbour just ahead, I flicked on my turn signal. Far below, the dark blue sea looked smooth as pressed satin, a sign the afternoon winds hadn't picked up. I'd been driving in the shade with my windows rolled down, enjoying the pleasant warmth. As I left the highway and emerged into sunshine, it was as if someone flipped the thermostat's switch. Instant hot. I pushed my hair off my neck, glad that home and Geoff were less than a minute away.

Unfortunately, so was Danny-Boy. He was waiting when we entered the shop's back door, practically filling Dunmaglass's cramped back room. He shouldn't have been there. Customers weren't allowed past the front showroom.

"How could you do that?" He glowered down on me, crowding me, backing me out of my own building.

Geoff inserted himself into the crevice between us. Putting his hand on Murdock's broad chest, he pushed hard. "Back off."

Murdock sneered at Geoff's hand as though it was no more threatening than a housefly, but complied. "I want an explanation."

"For what?" Geoff asked.

"I heard you're leaving Wee Claude's position as parade marshal empty."

Who told him? I peered around Geoff. "It was the committee's decision. We felt it expressed respect."

"Respect for whom?"

"Claude. Carrie." I cleared my throat, wishing my voice didn't sound so thin. "The committee felt—"

"I talked to every member of the Steering Committee and everyone agreed I was the best choice for replacement."

"Yes, if we needed a replacement." I nervously ducked behind Geoff, peeked around his other side. "But they decided instead to leave the position vacant this year."

"You mean to tell me Carrie Hunter's all right with breaking a two-hundred-year-old tradition?"

I didn't think it helpful to correct his miscount. "She was moved by the Steering Committee's decision."

Huffing angrily, Murdock plowed his fist into the rough wall. He left skin and blood on the stone. "Every time, every time I think I'm gonna get a break, it happens again!"

"What happens?"

"He's dead, and he's still doing it!"

"Doing what?"

"Wrecking my life! I thought I had the championship in the bag after Wee's accident. But no. A couple weeks and the guy's back competing, more determined than ever."

"Some people didn't think it was an accident," I said, ready to duck back behind Geoff.

He sucked on his bloody knuckles, making an apparent effort to control his temper. "How many times do I have to say that I liked the guy? Sure his conversion gig wore a little thin after a while, but I honestly liked him. Everybody did. So why would I hurt him?"

We didn't say anything.

"There's no percentage in it. I'd get kicked out of competition myself."

I inched around Geoff. "I'm sorry about the parade, really I am."

"Yeah. Like Highland Breweries is sorry."

"I thought Wee Claude arranged for them to sign you as their new spokesperson."

Geoff gave me a querying look, no doubt wondering where I'd heard that. Now wasn't the time to share my car conversation with Josh.

Danny-Boy pressed his injured knuckles against his thigh. "Claude said I was on the top of their list after he pulled out of his contract."

From Danny-Boy's frustrated tone, it seemed the deal had fallen through. "What happened?"

"Someone told them about Friday night!"

Geoff shifted so he was between us, again. "Friday?"

"There's never anyone along the shore road when it's foggy, but there were more cops than mosquitoes on Friday night. Pulled me over, and charged me with drunk driving."

"I warned you, with all the out-of-towners here for Claude's memorial, police would be making extra-sure nothing happened."

"So you're saying I did it to myself? 'Cause there's no way Highland Breweries is going to hire me to endorse their product. Not now."

"What are you going to do?" I asked.

"What can I do? Highland says they've started negotiations with some Scottish Heavyweight—as if he could better sell beer to Canadians. I'm out of the running no matter what!"

"I'm sorry," I said, again.

Danny-Boy fixed me with his narrow-eyed glare. "You think an apology will fix it?"

Nothing would fix it, not to Danny-Boy's satisfaction.

"Why did you come here?" Geoff asked. "You know there's nothing we can do."

"I thought if I was parade marshal they'd take my bid more seriously. Now? Maybe if Carrie talked to Highland? Explained how we're all broke up over Claude and doing dumb things? That the committee's decision had nothing to do with my driving conviction? "

"This isn't grade school. You can't send a note to the principal's office and expect your troubles to disappear," Geoff said.

"Then she should pay me for the lost revenue."

"She runs a toy store," I said. "How lucrative do you imagine that is?"

"Well, I'm not gonna sit around and do nothing." He elbowed Geoff out of the way. Not bothering to look back, he stormed across the street to where he'd parked his car.

"Should I warn Carrie that Danny-Boy's on the rampage?"

29

Danny-Boy's car disappeared around the corner, spewing gravel in its wake.

I said, "I'd better warn Carrie."

"It might be wiser to call your brother."

"And sic the cops on Danny-Boy for the second time in less than a week?" I fished in my purse for my cell phone and punched in Carrie's number.

"Maybe if I'd called Andrew the other night, after he punched Claude, he wouldn't have gone back later."

I touched his arm. "Josh said Claude was fine."

"Sure, when Danny-Boy arrived. But did he say anything about Claude's condition after Danny-Boy left the second time?"

Carrie wasn't picking up. "Josh said they parted amicably. Do you think she's at her mom's?"

"Could be. Josh said amicably?"

"That's my version of what he said. Point is, Danny-Boy and Wee Claude were still on pleasant speaking terms." I left Carrie a message. If she was visiting her mom, she'd get it when she got home. Maybe I should go by her house and make sure.

Geoff leaned against the wall. Arms folded across his chest, eyes closed, he let out a long breath. The lines bracketing his mouth slowly faded. He had such a lovely face—rugged, strong nosed. With his eyes closed, his eyelashes formed star-like points against his cheeks. It gave an unexpected softness to a man who seemed carved in sun-dried wood. God had searched the whole world to answer my prayers for a marriage-partner and brought this amazing man back into my life. I'd never imagined Geoff Grant could be God's choice for me.

I was so grateful he was.

Without opening his eyes, Geoff drew me close.

I rested my head against his chest and listened to the steady rhythm of his heart. Little by little my own slowed until it matched his. I love you, I sighed inwardly. I love you so much.

"Maybe you two should get a room." Ash's sarcasm obliterated my romantic mood. "There's a phone call for you," she continued. "And a bunch of messages from your Harbour Daze committee people."

"Now what?"

Once again, my hope for quiet time with God disappeared before it even had a chance. As for running by Carrie's, Geoff agreed to do a quick drive-by to ensure all was well at Hunter Hall, while I answered the phone.

The call was Mom. She'd made an extra-large batch of potato salad and wanted to know if Geoff and I'd like to come for supper. I said sure. Geoff loved Mom's invitations and accepted even when I was otherwise occupied. Which I was not. The waiting messages Ash warned me about could wait a little longer.

Consider my surprise when, fifteen minutes later, we strolled into Mom's kitchen and found Andrew and Inspector LeClerc sitting at the table snapping the tops off green beans. They tossed the beheaded veggies into a giant bowl—it was almost full—and the unwanted bits into a smaller one.

Mom lifted a bubbling, golden-crusted pie from the oven. Peach pie, if my scent-detector was working properly.

Geoff smacked his lips. "I claim the pie. What's everyone else going to eat?"

Mom considered it her life's mission to fatten Geoff. He was too thin, she'd said so many times I suspected Geoff half believed her. He was not too thin, of course. He was perfect. He'd be perfect after she fattened him up, too.

I smiled as he and Mom danced around the kitchen, Geoff trying to snatch a pie while she pretended to fend him off.

A frown dipped the corners of Inspector LeClerc's mouth. "She promised this pie to me," he said. "I may have to arrest you if you insist on commandeering what is rightfully mine."

Mom's cheeks pinked with pleasure. "Boys, boys," she used her best school teacher voice, "there's more than enough for everyone." Two other pies cooled on the rack.

Andrew, Geoff, and LeClerc exchanged greedy glances, obviously disputing the 'more than enough' part of her comment. It looked like I would have to fight for my fair share tonight.

Mom dumped the beans into a pot, rinsed them, and set the pot on the burner. "Tell your sister what you told me," she said.

I looked at Andrew, the only person with a sister in the room.

"This isn't the time."

"Fiddlesticks. Your father will come barging in here at any moment. You want to discuss this during supper?"

"Mom."

"Listen to your mama," said LeClerc. I wasn't sure if he agreed with Mom or was lobbying for a larger share of pie.

She wiped her hands on her apron. "Raoul agrees with me."

"Perhaps Gai-Lynn has insights." His accent gave my name an exotic lilt. "She knows the woman well. No?"

Andrew hushed me with his glare. "She barely knows the Hunters. It's pointless pumping Gai for information, or insights."

"She has spent two nights caring for Madame Oui—or Hunter, as you call her."

Mom nodded. "And we both know Gailynn's propensity for snooping."

"Gee, thanks, Mom." I began setting the table.

Andrew faced LeClerc with earnest eyes. "Raoul. Inspector. You don't know my sister. If you give Gai even the slightest hint of what you're after, she will take that and run with it. She'll pry. She'll accuse. She'll manufacture evidence."

"I do not manufacture evidence! OK, maybe I've been known to misinterpret what I've heard. Or get carried away with a theory. I won't deny that in the past I have stuck my nose where it's not appreciated. But I learned my lesson. I've changed." I turned to Geoff for support.

"Gai is under the impression that Danny-Boy Murdock harbors unreciprocated affection for Carrie," Geoff said.

I slapped down cutlery beside each plate.

Andrew's lips moved as he silently beseeched the

ceiling for wisdom, while LeClerc studied me through clear, perhaps even shrewd, eyes. He was, after all, an RCMP inspector.

"Is this so, Gai-Lynn?"

I offered him a tentative smile. Answering the question would prove Andrew's point, not mine. "It's a theory I've been working on. This morning I checked some old photos from the university, the local papers, that kind of thing, and I mean, I understand this is all open for interpretation, and my interpretations could be wrong. They've been wrong before. But I've found several pictures—well, maybe three isn't exactly several—where it looks to me like Danny-Boy's fixated on Carrie, while everyone else in the picture is looking at Claude. Claude was very charismatic, in the secular sense of the word." I glanced at Andrew, Mom, and Geoff.

"So, you suggest Danny-Boy Murdock had another reason for wanting Claude Oui out of the running." LeClerc appeared to consider my theory. "I will need to see these pictures. Get them from your sister," he told Andrew. "We will look at them tonight."

Dad arrived, and the discussion was abandoned.

Geoff headed out as soon as he'd eaten dessert. He had a church committee meeting for something or other. Inspector LeClerc, Raoul, as he insisted we call him, left at the same time. He had paperwork to do. I planned to help Mom with the dishes, but Andrew pulled me aside before I'd finished clearing the table and led me out to the driveway.

"OK, here's the deal. We walk to your place, you give me the pictures, and then you're out of it. Understand?"

"I'm trying." I quickened my pace to match his strides. "I can't help it, though, if I hear something or see something that makes me wonder. I can't just turn off my brain—no matter what you think."

"I'm not saying turn off your brain. Sometimes it works."

I almost tripped over his backhanded compliment.

"Telling me about Josh, that was good. And, if your hunch about Danny-Boy holds water, we'll call that good brain-work too."

"If?"

"Not convinced his rivalry with Wee Claude was anything more than hoopla. Athletes do it all the time. Gets the fans worked up."

"Mom said Carrie and Danny-Boy were an item a long time ago."

"Ancient history." He held up his hand. "But I'll look into it."

I found myself standing taller, hearing Andrew actually consider one of my theories. "But what should I do about Danny-Boy? He keeps popping up, wanting me to intervene. He wants to see Carrie, even though I know she doesn't want to see him. I'm turning into a buffer between the two, and I don't want to be."

"Then don't."

I grabbed his arm, making his slow down and look at me. "How do I avoid it?"

"Wash your hands of the two."

"And leave Carrie alone? She has no one other than her cranky old mom in Antigonish. Can you imagine? Carrie and I may not be kindred spirits, but I can't just walk away. Not while she's grieving. Besides, what if Danny-Boy is Claude's killer? You expect me to stand back and let him have at her?"

"It's not like you could stop him."

"So what are you saying I should do?"

He scratched his head, as if this was a real puzzler. "Call me? Look, Carrie's a big girl. Sounds harsh, but you don't want to turn into her crutch."

"Someone broke into her house, stole her frogs, and killed her husband. If you don't want me involved, find out who did all that. Then she won't need a crutch."

Andrew's spine straightened, a sign our companionable chat was over. "You know I can't discuss an ongoing investigation."

I threw up my hands. "Then what were we just doing?"

"That, sister-dear, was me, *cop*"—he did finger quotations when he said cop—"telling you, *civilian,*"—again with the finger quotes—"to keep your nose out of official police business."

We'd reached Dunmaglass. I let us in, and Andrew followed me upstairs to my little office. I hated giving him the satisfaction of stepping back from the investigation, but I hadn't much choice. To do otherwise, was me being a nosy, meddlesome snoop. And at twenty-five, I was too young to be a meddlesome snoop. In a way, I even felt relieved. Once I finished my Hum Harbour Daze responsibilities, I'd be back on track with work, jewelry making, and wedding plans.

With that in mind, I printed off the three photos I'd found online, handed them to Andrew, and bid silent farewell to my sleuthing days. The shore and a quiet, celebratory walk beckoned.

Wind pleated the harbor as I wandered slowly down the curve of shore. The beach was a mix of sand

and smooth tumbled stones, and at this time of day, when the sun had disappeared behind the hills, the harbor, the beach, the surrounding slopes, were a shadowless grey. Colored glass was impossible to spot. Which didn't matter. After the tumultuous day, I was searching the shore for peace, not bits of sea-tumbled glass.

I wiped everything from my mind. Murder—gone. Frog thief—gone. Andrew, Carrie, Danny-Boy—gone. Even Geoff—gone. Sort of. The soothing rumble of the waves. The familiar smells of salt water and cut wood of the lumber yard. The rhythm of my breaths, the crunch of my footsteps.

I listened for the Still Small Voice of Peace.

I heard His sigh.

I was content.

Then I remembered that late night argument between Carrie and Black Hair, which I'd forgotten to mention to Andrew.

30

Geoff's lights were on by the time I got back from my walk. I crossed from my place to his and rapped on his sliding door. Sheba followed me inside. Since Geoff and I had become a pair, she considered both apartments home.

He poured sugar and milk into a mug and handed me the doctored coffee. "Could you have misinterpreted?" he asked told him what I'd seen.

"They argued. Carrie cried. They hugged."

"Did they kiss?"

"I wasn't going to hang around and wait for it."

"So the hug could have been platonic?"

I replayed the scene in my mind. "He didn't seem in a hurry to hold her."

Geoff leaned against the kitchen counter, his mug in his hand.

I inhaled the fumes from mine. "I should tell Andrew."

"Any idea who the guy is?"

"I can't help wondering if he has something to do with Claude's death. I mean, he was never here before Claude died."

Geoff set down his mug, took mine, and put it beside his. He led me into the living room and pulled me down into his recliner with him. "Don't go jumping to conclusions. That's what gets you into trouble."

"I'm not jumping. I'm simply stating a verifiable

fact."

"This guy being in Hum Harbour may be connected to Claude's death, but that doesn't necessarily mean he is."

"How do we find out?"

"We don't. Remember? That's police business."

I rested my head against his shoulder. "Can't I be curious about someone new in town?"

Geoff's arm tightened around me. "Where is he staying?"

"Do you think he's sleeping at Carrie's? She hasn't asked me to stay over since the memorial."

"I didn't see him at the memorial."

"Well, he was at Hunter Hall for the reception. I caught him upstairs looking for the bathroom."

Geoff hmphed.

"I didn't think anything about it at the time. There were so many people I didn't know, and it sounded reasonable. The bathroom demand was brisk."

"Could he be related to her?"

I'd wondered that, myself. "She's never mentioned relatives coming from away."

"And Claude's family cut him off years ago."

Sheba butted my knee, and I shifted to make room for her on my lap. "What could he have done to deserve that?"

"He never talked about his life before Carrie. I assumed he was ashamed of where he'd come from."

"Compared to the Hunters?"

He threaded his fingers through mine. "Wealth has a way of shaming the poor."

"What was it Carrie said? 'You stop noticing the things that are always with you.' I wonder if he regretted sacrificing his family for her?"

"He loved her."

"He kept a journal, you know."

"Gai."

"I found it in his home office." Sheba stepped from my lap to Geoff's and lay down. Apparently his was more comfortable. "Maybe it explains why he's estranged from his family."

"It'll be in police custody."

"Of course it will." Except it was still beside Claude's chair after the police had bagged, tagged, and taken away their evidence. And as far as I knew they'd not come back for more. Maybe I should mention it to Andrew. Or I could ask Carrie.

****

Tuesday morning I played catch-up at the clinic. Geoff had a full morning booked, and the waiting room hummed with people coming and going. At exactly ten-o-six—the clock on the wall was right across from my desk so I couldn't miss it—the clinic door banged open, and my cousin Ash marched in.

She slammed a piece of loose leaf on top of my computer keyboard, sending a zillion unconnected letters skittering across the screen. "I quit," she said loud enough to turn heads. "Effective immediately. There's my r-resignation."

I picked up the page. It said "I quit effective immediately" in her left-sloping script.

I took a deep breath and told myself not to panic. Surely whatever'd upset her was fixable. I mean, she couldn't quit now, not with Hum Harbour Daze, the shops' busiest season, only days away. "What's wrong?"

"You had no right sticking your nose in my business!"

I half stood. "Is everything at Dunmaglass all right?"

"D-dunmaglass? Is that all you care about?"

Geoff poked his head out of the examining room. "Is everything all right out here?"

"No!" snapped Ash. "It's not all right."

"Maybe you should keep your voice down," I said.

"I will n-not!"

"Gailynn, could you please take your cousin outside and deal with whatever is wrong?" Geoff phrased it as a question, but I knew it wasn't.

I came around the desk, took Ash's elbow, and ushered her to the door, smiling reassuringly to the folks in the waiting room who, I'm sure, would have preferred we stay so they could hear what Ash had to say. Once I'd herded Ash out the door, I latched it firmly behind us, and propelled her up the street. Away from prying ears.

"What is with you?" I demanded. "You can't just march into a place of business and start shouting at people. If you have a problem—"

"If I have a problem? If? Oh, that's s-s-sweet."

"Stop ranting and explain."

"As if you don't know?"

"I don't know!"

"B-baloney!"

"Ashleigh Margaret MacDonald, stop this melodramatic twaddle, and tell me what's happened!"

"Josh b-broke up with me!"

Mrs. MacPhee peered at us between her front curtains. I smiled and waved all was well. "When did he do that?"

"This morning while I was opening your stupid Dunmaglass, he came in and said he c-couldn't see me anymore."

Had he spoken to Andrew, too?

"What's happened?"

She caught the tip of her index finger between her front teeth and tore off a length of fingernail. "He said you called him cheap and inconsiderate and un-t-trustworthy."

"Well…"

"How could you? Josh is the b-best thing that's ever happened to me."

"Ash, he breaks into people's houses and steals things."

"For me."

"You asked him to do it?"

She tore a strip off another nail. "Of course I never asked him to steal kitchen f-frogs. But he's done it because he loves me. And you've ruined it."

"I've ruined it?" I almost sputtered. "I'm the one who's been covering for him because I didn't want you hurt."

"So that's why you c-called him names and threatened to go to the police?"

"Ash." I said her name softly, trying to damp down the anger factor. "Have you considered the possibility that Josh has done more than swipe a few dozen kitchen frogs?"

"Like what?"

"He was at Hunter Hall the night Claude Oui died."

Ash placed her hands on her hips. "S-so."

"There are a number of pricey folk art frogs missing from Carrie Hunter's collection."

"You think Josh took them?"

I spread my hands.

"If he took them, he'd have given them t-to me, and he hasn't."

"Maybe he's holding them until things cool down?"

"Since I know, for a fact, he never took Carrie Hunter's yuppie folk art frogs, the answer is no. He's not holding them until things c-cool down."

"How do you know Josh doesn't have them?"

"Because he told me so. And Josh doesn't lie to me."

"You knew he'd been stealing kitchen frogs for you?"

"No. But he never l-lied about it once I asked him."

"And you asked if he's got Carrie's missing collectables?"

"He said, 'I don't have Carrie Hunter's stuff.' Direct quote. Good enough?"

"Then why did he break up with you?"

"Because you made him feel like he wasn't good enough. People are always treating him like he's less than they are. I'm not surprised when some people do that, b-but you? I thought you were different."

"Hold it. Are you trying to turn this around and say I'm prejudiced?"

"If the shoe fits."

I stuck my finger in her face. "Don't you ever, ever, accuse me of treating him badly because he looks different than I do. I've lived my entire life being different. Having people look at me and whisper." As the only non-redhead in three generations of MacDonalds, my black hair stirred a lot of tongues, not just Phyllis Hunter's. It wasn't until a teacher questioned my parentage in front of my entire class that my dad pulled out some old family photos of my great-grandmother, a Mi'kmaq whom I closely resemble, that my own doubts began to fade.

"This has nothing to do with what he's like on the outside and everything to do with what he's like on the inside. You"—I poked her—"you deserve a man you can trust. Anyone who sneaks into people's houses, and takes things that don't belong to them, I don't care what their reason, is not trustworthy."

Her eyes filled with tears. "But I love him."

"Then convince him to do the right thing."

"You want Josh to t-turn himself in?"

"I want Josh to be the kind of man God intended him to be—an honest one."

She swiped her tears away with the back of her hand. "I've got to find him."

"Head back to Dunmaglass, and by the time you close up tonight, I'm sure he'll have reconsidered."

She hiked her purse up on her shoulder. "You've got my resignation. I'm not coming back to Dunmaglass unless Josh and I get b-back together."

"But I need you."

"Now you know what it feels like."

31

Between patients, I explained the crisis to Geoff. He wasn't as concerned as I about Dunmaglass's closure. "We'll work it out," he promised.

I nodded. Four days. That's how long I had to convince Ash to come back to work. And if I didn't, Dunmaglass would be closed during Hum Harbour Daze, and the shop's bottom line would be so low I might as well bury it.

****

Once the clinic closed, I spent the afternoon manning my shop. I had half a dozen walk-ins and three sales. Not bad.

Reverend Innes dropped by to say he'd been unable to find a new space to house Hum Harbour Daze crafters' and farmers' market. He'd tried the church hall, the Legion, and the community center—all were too small by themselves, but he thought if he divided the vendors between all three buildings, it might work.

Unfortunately, all three had been spoken for by other festival participants.

Reverend Innes tugged his dress Stuart vest. "I've run out of options. I'm afraid we may have to cancel the whole market."

I gaped in disbelief. "Cancel? The craft sale and

farmer's market's almost as big a draw as the lobster boat races."

"We're running out of time, and I don't see an alternative."

"Why can't we rent a tent?"

He looked doubtful. "How? Where would you even begin to look?"

"The internet."

"I can barely figure out emails. And I can't very well ask Vi. Between work and her Steering Committee activities, I can't expect her to do this, too." His eyes brightened. "But you could find out."

"Me?"

"You're chair of the Steering Committee."

"I chaired one meeting to oversee the parade marshal decision."

He patted his vest. "Apparently you were promoted."

"I mean, I'm OK with helping Carrie, but I'm not in charge."

"You should talk to her. Because that's the clear signal we're getting any time one of us has a question or a detail that needs ironing out. She says 'Ask Gailynn.'"

"That's insane." I checked my watch. Running over to Carrie's now would mean closing the shop early, which I hated to do. But I needed to sort out this misunderstanding pronto. "I'll talk to Carrie and get back to you."

"As long as I don't run out of the time needed to notify the vendors they shouldn't bother coming because there's no place for them to set up, I really don't need the details."

"Of course you do," I said. "You're the events

coordinator."

He tilted his head, a weary expression on his face as he studied me. "You don't understand, do you, Gailynn?"

I must have looked blank.

"The committee's a formality. The Hunters do all the work for Hum Harbour Daze. It's always been that way. It always will be."

I felt my stomach plummet. "Carrie can't handle it this year. Not after losing her husband."

"That's why she picked you."

****

As soon as I locked up, I made a beeline for Hunter Hall.

Carrie'd hung the CLOSED sign in the front door's window, meaning both Hunter Monuments and Toys were unavailable for business. I tried the door knob—locked—and rang the bell.

Cupping my face against the glass, I could see clear through to the back of the house, where Carrie sat at the kitchen table. "Carrie, it's me. We need to talk." I tapped on the widow and waved.

She jumped, as though surprised to see me. Pushing back her chair, she walked unevenly to the door and let me in. She glanced up and down the street then locked it behind me.

"You've closed Dunmaglass early? No wait, your cousin is looking after it for you."

"Not at the moment," I said. "But that's not why I'm here."

She stooped, bringing her eyes level with mine. "Why are you here?" She pushed her uncombed hair out of her eyes.

I sniffed discreetly, wondering if I would detect the smell of liquor on her breath. I didn't. But I thought I scented cigarette lingering in the air.

"I haven't been drinking," she said. "If that's what you're thinking."

"I wasn't."

"Of course you were. Just like people thought Claude drank."

"I know he didn't."

"Good for you, because I wasn't always sure. And I'm the one who was supposed to believe in him."

I'd been hearing a lot of people talk about Claude, good things and bad. Despite all the recent press Post Concussion Syndrome was receiving, they were still unfamiliar with PCS symptoms. They misinterpreted what they saw, and drew erroneous conclusions.

I took Carrie's elbow, and led her back to the kitchen table covered with invoices and bills. I also recognized Claude's leather-bound journal. Good. Perhaps I could learn if it mentioned Claude's absentee family.

"Can I make you some tea?" You'd think it was my kitchen, not hers.

She braced her head in her hands. "I'm sick of tea. I'm sick of charity casseroles. And I'm sick of sympathy baking. I wish everything would just go back to the way it was."

"You miss him." I took a breath. "Does reading his journal help?"

She ignored my question. "I thought I loved this place, you know? The great Hunter Hall with all its heritage. It's a mausoleum. I know people say that." She shrugged. "So I fill it with frogs. Frogs are quirky.

Frogs are cute. Frogs make the place…better. You know?"

I nodded, even though I didn't agree.

"Claude was good with my frogs." She raked her fingers through her hair and twisted it into a messy knot at the back of her head. "Your brother and that French inspector were here this afternoon."

I sat in the chair opposite Carrie.

"They've decided Claude was killed with my frog candlestick." She shook her head back and forth, back and forth. I'm not sure she realized she was doing it.

"Did they say he was killed with the candlestick they took from the house?"

"That one was clean."

She obviously knew more about the official investigation than I did. "Then the murderer took the other candlestick with him?"

"And some of my frogs to cover up the loss."

"Is that what Andrew said?"

"Your brother wouldn't say anything. Just the inspector." She looked at me sharply. "Why do we need to talk?"

I dragged my brain from discussions of murder to Hum Harbour Daze and the reason I'd come. "The members of the Steering Committee seem to be under the mistaken impression that I'm in charge of the festival."

"Mistaken? I thought you agreed to take over."

"I agreed to chair one meeting."

She shook her head emphatically. "I distinctly recall asking you to assume responsibility for overseeing things this year. You did say you'd do anything."

"To help you. But now people are expecting me to

do their jobs, too."

"So you want me to do them?"

"No." I stared at the scattered papers and Claude's journal in consternation. "But I think people should do the jobs they agreed to do."

"So do I."

I was caught. How could I demand others hold up their end of things if I didn't hold up mine? Although I still wasn't convinced I'd ever committed to holding up my end. I looked at her closely. Was she really putting me in charge?

"You mean I have final say on any issue that arises?"

"You're responsible."

"If we have to rent a tent for the crafters?"

She spread her hands. "As long as you stay within budget."

I vaguely wondered what would happened if I didn't. "Is there a checklist of all the things you've done in past years? It'd help if I had something like that."

She riffled through the papers on the table, maybe expecting to find a list among them. "Must be upstairs. I'll see what I can find." Before she left me, taking Claude's journal with her, she shoved the papers into a manila folder, and stuffed the folder into a drawer.

I seemed powerless to tear my gaze from that drawer. Why did she hide her papers before leaving the room? For privacy or secrecy?

The French doors opened onto the patio and her beloved garden beyond. The plants she moved the other day drooped in their new location. No doubt she'd be moving them back to where they started. Or the compost pile in the back corner.

I squirted dish soap and water into the sink and washed the stack of dirty dishes. I dried them and put them away.

I spotted a loose paper on the floor, part of the bill collection she hadn't wanted me to see? I crawled under the table to retrieve it and slid it into the manila folder in the drawer. In the process, however, I inadvertently saw what it was. Phyllis Hunter's monthly statement from the Inverness Arms. $7500 per month. Is that what people paid to live in a seniors' care facility?

Carrie reappeared with my list. I'd arrived at her door anxious to dispel the idea that I was in charge of Hum Harbour Daze. Instead, I now held a seven-page document detailing—I scanned it quickly--everything from stocking toilet paper in the portable toilets to stocking snack foods for the band—that I was responsible for.

"Gai--" she'd never before shortened my name to the familiar "--I have one more favor to ask."

I swallowed. Look what the last favor had turned into.

She handed me her precious necklace. "I snagged it somehow when I pulled off my sweater last night. I broke the clasp. With your jewelry skills, can you repair it for me?"

Snagged it on her sweater? Last night? I studied the clasp, hoping she didn't see the disbelief on my face.

"It's not the kind I usually work with, but I don't suppose it should be too hard to fix. Or I can replace it, if it's not repairable."

"Thank you." She smiled at me for the first time since I found her doing CPR on Claude's lifeless body.

32

With Carrie's gorgeous necklace safely stowed in a little velvet bag in my jeans pocket and the mega-list rolled up in my hand, I took the beach way home. There was a strong chop in the water, the kind that smashed loudly against the shore, drowning out any sounds from town or the wharf. It gave you a false sense of being alone, which I appreciated.

I had much to ponder.

If Claude had been bludgeoned with Carrie's candlestick in the midst of a frog robbery, the chance of the thief being the murderer jumped a thousand percent. Thank goodness it wasn't Josh. He swore he'd never been inside Hunter Hall. Thing was, I really didn't believe him. Which meant Josh lied and could still be our killer.

On the other hand, I honestly couldn't picture Josh as a killer. Even if Claude caught him red-handed, I couldn't see the kid lashing out like that. As for Claude, if he'd caught Josh stealing, he would have talked the kid into giving everything back and probably had him praying the sinner's prayer before he went home.

Would Andrew and Inspector LeClerc see it that way? Or would they haul Josh in as their most likely suspect? Maybe they already had.

No wonder Ash was furious with me.

The sun beat hot on my head. I found a log that

had washed up on the beach and sat on it. I needed to find a way to prove Josh's innocence. Not that he'd trust me after I called him cheap, inconsiderate, and untrustworthy. I'd meant it in love.

I snorted. Who was I trying to fool?

I poked at the sand. If I convinced Ash that I wanted to help, maybe she could convince Josh. Except Josh had broken ties with Ash, might even be in custody at this very moment, so how would she convince him of anything if she couldn't even talk to him?

Man, I'd made a mess of things. Tears of self pity stung my eyes.

Geoff would help clear things up. I know I had only to ask, but I hated to go to him, to admit what I'd done. To see the disappointment in his face.

I scrubbed at my tears.

And what if Geoff couldn't fix it? What if the evidence, circumstantial though it was, satisfied police enough that they quit hunting for Claude's real killer and set their sights on Josh?

What if poor Josh ran away because he knew police were about to charge him with murder? Or, what if he believed he'd be arrested and did something worse? He was just a kid, after all. Kids did dumb things. They reacted; they didn't think about consequences. The police could use all those reasons to justify their case against Josh.

This wasn't good.

Cresting waves smashed against the beach, sending spray into the air.

I wiped my nose with the front of my t-shirt.

Fifteen, maybe twenty feet from shore, something red bucked in the water. It surfaced, seemed to roll over, and disappeared. It didn't look solid, like a buoy. It looked like fabric, swelling, shrinking back against whatever it covered.

What it covered looked like a shoulder.

I stood. It, he, whatever was out there, rolled closer, before dipping beneath the water again.

I'd been sitting here wondering if Josh might do something destructive and now it looked as if someone had.

I spun around, looking for anyone who could help. Twice I'd almost drowned. I knew how deadly the sea could be. Nothing, nothing was more terrifying than the ocean. It closed over your head, dragging you down to where there was no air, no breath, no light. I retched.

I watched the red.

Someone needed to wade into that churning swell, and pull whatever…whoever that was, to shore.

"Help!" I ran in a circle. "Help! Someone help me!"

No one came.

God, you have to send help. I stumbled toward the water's edge, but when the breaking wave clawed up the beach, I scurried back in terror. The red sank from view.

I spun again, my eyes aching to find someone, anyone, who would run into the water and save the red.

But there was no one. Only me.

Lord have mercy, I had no choice.

"Help me," I shouted at God. I coughed up bile as I put one foot after the other and forced myself into the swell.

It sucked the ground from beneath my feet and

shoved me back. The red reappeared and sank. I stumbled further into the water. Within feet, I was past my waist, the waves slamming my chest, soaking my face.

I screamed at God. I reached. I strained. My fingers touched fabric, and I grabbed.

I fought my way back to shore, and the red came with me. Willingly.

I lost my footing and almost washed back into the harbor. But the wave receded, and it wasn't that deep after all.

The next wave slammed against the back of my head. On hands and knees, I crawled up the sloping beach, dragging the red behind me, until both of us were safe from being sucked back to sea.

That's when I rolled over and saw the entire red for the first time.

It wasn't a body. It was a sack.

33

Geoff found me huddled against my log, sopping wet, shivering. I'd made no attempt to open the red sack.

He hunkered down and gathered me into his arms. Slowly his heat penetrated my fright, and the shivering subsided.

"What were you thinking?" he asked. Geoff knew how I felt about water. Aquaphobia, he called it, though I'm not sure my cowardice deserved a clinical designation.

"I thought it was Josh."

I felt him look around. "The sack?"

"It's red."

"And you thought…oh, Gai." He hugged me tighter. "That's the bravest thing I've ever known anyone to do."

"It's not Josh."

"No, sweetheart, it's not Josh. He's at my apartment, with Ash. She's trying to convince him to tell Andrew what he saw the other night."

"What did he see?"

"I have no idea. I don't think Ash does, either. She just knows if they're going to have any kind of a future, he has to take responsibility for his actions."

"Isn't that what Claude always said? There's no forgiveness until we take responsibility for our sins?"

He kissed my soggy hair. "Are you ready to go

home?"

I crawled out of his lap. My clothes clung to me like second skin. I plucked at my t-shirt.

"Come on." Taking my hand he pulled me to my feet. "No one will see you."

I slid under his waiting arm. "Don't forget the sack. I almost died for that thing." He didn't contradict me, though I'm sure he thought I was being melodramatic, and hoisted the sack over his shoulder.

Geoff waited while I showered and changed, then we crossed the bridge to his place. He left the red sack on his terrace and slid open his door for me to enter first. Ash and Josh were still there. They sat at opposite ends of the couch, and judging by their mutinous expressions, I'd say they'd been arguing.

"He refuses," said Ash.

Josh stuck out his chin. "I'm not sticking my neck in a noose."

"It's not a noose if you're t-telling the truth."

"You think I'm lying?"

Obviously, they'd resolved nothing, but at least they were talking—well, shouting—and Josh wasn't out doing worse.

Geoff offered me the recliner and pulled up a kitchen chair for himself. "I may have something that will tip the scales."

"How?" asked Ash.

Josh watched Geoff. Suspiciously?

"Gai rescued something from the harbor. Thought you might like to see it." Without waiting for their answer—Josh and Ash exchanged glances, hers curious, his worried?—Geoff retrieved the red sack from outside.

He dropped it on the coffee table, unconcerned

with the wet stain it would leave.

Now that I was no longer in a panic and could think and see rationally, I could tell this was not and should never have been mistaken for a person. It was a faded Montreal Canadiens pillowcase, mostly red, with the distinctive blue and white logo. When I'd dragged it up the beach, I was pretty sure the end had been securely knotted. It wasn't now. Geoff must have opened it while I showered.

Seeing the soggy pillowcase, Josh began scratching his head.

Ash gave me the raised eyebrow.

"Would you like to see what's inside?" asked Geoff.

She scooted toward the middle of the couch and leaned forward.

Josh pressed himself as far away as possible without falling on the floor.

My own curiosity intensified by his response to the pillowcase, I knelt beside the coffee table, eager for the big reveal.

Indulging the drama of the moment, Geoff slowly reached into the pillowcase. His arm disappeared up to his elbow. The fabric quivered. He lifted out the first object and placed it carefully on the table.

It was one of Carrie's frogs. I'd have staked my life on it.

Geoff reached into the pillowcase and brought out a second and a third, until the pillowcase was empty, and a row of frog figurines stretched the length of the coffee table.

We all stared at them.

"Are those…?" Ash looked at me.

"Carrie's? Yep."

Tentatively, fingers extended, Ash caressed the largest figurine—a crowned frog standing on his back legs as he, lips puckered, strained towards, well, presumably the princess. "It's b-beautiful," she whispered. Her face glowing with awe, she crouched beside the table and studied each one. Except for the frog prince, she didn't touch any.

Josh seemed unable to drag his gaze from Ash's rapt face.

"Oh, Josh." She turned to him, her eyes filled with tears. "You d-did this for me?" She threw herself into his arms, and they spilled onto the floor. He laughed. She cried.

Geoff and I looked at each other.

"We need to notify police that Carrie's stolen figurines have been retrieved," Geoff said. "I'm not sure they'll be able to get fingerprints off of them, apart from ours. They've been soaking in sea water for days. And the pillowcase is old. It could have come from anywhere."

Josh extricated himself from Ash. "You think?"

Geoff said, "I think you have a couple of different options. Gai and I can show these to Andrew. Gai found the pillowcase. Not knowing what was inside we opened it. This is what we discovered."

"All true," I said.

"Or we could tell Andrew and LeClerc the extended version."

"The extended version?" I imagined Josh paled when he said that.

"We keep with the original story I just said, but you're going to add your confession."

"My confession?" Josh's Adam's apple bobbed in his throat.

"That you took these figurines from Hunter Hall and, having realized the error of your ways, you are overcome by remorse for the additional pain you've caused Carrie on top of the death of her husband. So you threw them away. But now that they're back, you want to return them to her in good faith."

"Give 'em back?"

"They're going back either way. One way gets you off the hook and makes you look good in Ash's eyes. The other way leaves a lot of unanswered questions that aren't good for you."

"But they're gonna think I murdered Claude."

"Did you?"

Josh recoiled. "No!"

I wasn't being fooled a second time. "You lied before. Why should we believe you now? Why should Andrew?"

"I was scared. I lied because I knew what everybody'd think."

Hands on my hips, I narrowed the space between us. "And now we're thinking it. You robbed Hunter Hall. You killed Claude to cover it up."

"So I lied." Panic made his voice shrill. "That doesn't mean I killed him!"

"And I don't see the alleged murder weapon." Geoff's observation gave me pause.

The assorted frogs on the coffee table did not include the totem-like candlestick.

Geoff continued. "Don't take this the wrong way, Josh, but if you were the killer, I'd expect the murder weapon to be tucked into this pillowcase with the other frogs. You wouldn't think to dispose of it separately."

Josh nodded.

"So which will it be? Option one, or option two?"

Ash clasped his hand in both of hers and gazed imploringly into his eyes.

Who can resist young love? Josh's shoulders curled inward. "Call the cops."

34

Call the cops.

When you call the police you expect them to come running. After all, they are committed to serve and protect. You assume they'd do it immediately.

According to dispatch, however, Andrew and LeClerc were off tracking down some case-breaking lead and would get back to us when they returned. Hopefully tonight.

Geoff was reluctant to let Josh out of his sight while we waited. He thought the kid might chicken out on confessing and run, so he ordered pizza for us to share, and when it was ready I scooted downstairs to the Heron to pick it up. No need to pay delivery costs.

Geoff hung up the phone when I returned with supper. "Inverness Arms," he said. Someone had needed a medication change; fortunately, the job could be done over the phone.

We sat around Geoff's outdoor table—the inside one isn't big enough for four people—and gorged ourselves on seafood pizza and talked about Hum Harbour Daze. More specifically, how I'd ended up as the festival's troubleshooter when I had no idea what I was doing.

Josh said he knew someone who knew someone who worked for a guy who knew someone who'd rented a giant tent for some outdoor mattress event—truck loads of mismatched mattresses on sale cheap—

earlier in the summer. A few text messages later, I had a name and a phone number. I excused myself and called the mattress guy.

Mattress Guy told me he'd borrowed it from a buddy who, years before, had bought one for his daughter's wedding reception. The father-of-the-bride, when I called him, said he stored the disassembled tent in an old fish factory.

"I've promised it to a buddy for this weekend, but after that it's all yours."

"But I need it this weekend."

"Real sorry, missy, but this weekend's already spoken for. Where'd you say you were from?"

I couldn't hold back my sigh. Here came the traditional who-are-you-related-to conversation. "Hum Harbour."

"I don't know what Sam MacDonald wanted my tent for, but he's from Hum Harbour, ain't he? Maybe you can work out something with him."

"Sam?" My brother?

"Said he needed it for that big festival you got going. I come every year, you know. Love them lobster boat races. I never won, but always give it a shot. This year, though. I think I've got a good chance this year. My son-in-law's designed this new engine boost system…"

By the time I got back to the table, the pizza was gone and Geoff had pulled out Scrabble.

Andrew and Inspector LeClerc arrived as I was about to add "un" to "requited" for a big one-hundred-six points. It would have put me out front and possibly marked the first time I'd ever beaten Geoff at Scrabble. So much for that.

The two were filthy. I poured them glasses of iced

water while they took turns in the bathroom trying to clean up.

"Are we allowed to ask what you've been doing?"

"You may ask," said LeClerc after draining his glass. He spotted the frogs displayed on the coffee table and muttered something in French that sounded a lot like a swear word.

"Are these what I think they are?"

"If you think they're Carrie's missing frogs."

"Where did they come from?"

Josh gripped Ash's hand as he faced the inspector. "Gai found them washed up on the beach." OK, sorta true. "But they got there because I'd chucked them off the end of the wharf."

"When did you do that?"

"Saturday night. Right after I found Claude lying in the middle of the floor in his front hall."

Geoff shifted. That wasn't what he'd directed Josh to say.

"He had fallen?" asked LeClerc.

"I dunno if he fell or not."

"Did you try helping him?"

Josh's Adam's apple bobbed. "I touched him, if that's what you mean."

"How did you touch him?"

Geoff cleared his throat. "Look, I know you guys want answers, but this is not the statement Josh intended to make, and I'm going to suggest he stop answering until he calls his Dad and a lawyer."

LeClerc shrugged. "This is his right, of course, but we are just talking. No one is accusing him of anything."

Josh glanced between the two, panic registering in his face. "But you said if I told the truth—"

Geoff held up his hand. "I did. Telling the truth is always the best thing to do. But in light of what you just said—"

While Geoff talked, Ash pressed against Josh's side and whispered, "You really touched his body?"

"—I think it would be wisest for you to have an advocate with you while you tell the truth."

"But I can't afford no lawyer."

"I can" said Geoff. "Call your dad, and I'll call my lawyer, and when they're both here, you can tell Andrew and Inspector LeClerc everything you saw and heard."

Josh's dad arrived within minutes, his pajamas visible beneath his clothes. He seemed anxious for Josh to tell police everything he knew. "He doesn't need a lawyer. He's not being charged. No one's read him his rights, have they?"

Geoff herded Josh and Mr. Pry into the kitchen. "This isn't an American TV show. Our police don't adhere to American laws."

Mr. Pry sniffed derisively. "We still got laws here in Canada."

"But they're different. I personally do not know how they differ. I just know they do."

Mr. Pry looked at his son. Like Josh, his prominent Adam's apple bobbed whenever he swallowed, which he was doing often.

"Do you want to risk Josh's situation getting more complicated than it already is?" asked Geoff.

"This is my boy's life we're talking about."

"Then wait for the lawyer. He left Antigonish the same time you left your house."

Mr. Pry checked his watch. "He sure better be on his way like you said, 'cause I think holding out only makes Josh look more guilty." He saw me hovering in the doorway, trying to be a wall between them and the two cops in the living room.

"Geoff's a wise man, Mr. Pry. If he thinks it's in Josh's best interest to wait, then I can't see what harm it will do."

"Maybe we should wait for Josh's lawyer at the station," said LeClerc.

I tried to picture Andrew, Inspector LeClerc, Josh, Mr. Pry, and a lawyer, all squeezed into the tiny office at Hum Harbour's police station. Sardines in a can had more leg room. "Couldn't you talk here?"

"There is more space," said Andrew.

I said, "Ash and I'll leave. And when the lawyer arrives, Geoff can come over to my place, too. That way you'll have as much privacy as you would at the station but more room to breathe."

LeClerc hesitated. "MacDonald, you will take notes?"

Andrew produced a notepad and a pen. "Whatever you need."

"Then it is settled. Ladies…"

35

Ash and I watched an old, made-for-TV movie about a man-eating snake. Geoff arrived around the time the shirtless hero rescued the scantily-dressed heroine for the first time. By the end of the flick, he'd saved her a dozen times more. Then came the news, with the usual wars, earthquakes, and crime sprees. That American jewel thief was still at large, but our frog thief seemed to be flying under the radar.

We didn't talk. We just stared at the TV and wondered what was happening at Geoff's.

Andrew saved us from the late night talk shows when he tapped on the sliding door and let himself in. Wanting inside for the night, Sheba squeezed through with him.

"We're done," he said to Geoff. "You can go home now."

"And?" said Ash.

"And what?" Sometimes Andrew could be so obtuse.

"Josh? What's h-happened to Josh? Where is he?"

"On his way home with his dad, I expect. Unless they're detouring for a donut on the way."

"Home." Her eyes overflowed with tears as she sprang from the chair to hug Andrew.

He gave her a cousinly back pat. "What did I do?" he mouthed.

"You saved her man from incarceration."

"Long as Carrie's happy with her frogs back, and doesn't press charges."

Geoff heaved himself from the couch. "Then you don't think he had anything to do with Claude's death?"

"Like you said to LeClerc, if the kid was gonna toss the murder weapon, he'd toss it with the rest of the stuff he lifted."

"You told LeClerc that?" I slipped appreciative arms around Geoff's waist.

"It's a moot point, anyway," said Andrew. "We found the missing frog candlestick earlier this evening, and it wasn't anywhere near the beach."

"Where was it?"

"Sorry." Andrew grinned, knowing unsatisfied curiosity would keep me awake half the night. "Police business."

I whacked him with a throw pillow. That was what they were called.

He pitched it back. There was some lighthearted banter. Andrew offered to drive Ash home, and they left.

Geoff departed soon after.

I stood in the middle of the living room, suddenly too weary to move. My arms felt like they weighed a million pounds. Such relief. Josh would be OK.

But Claude's killer was still out there.

I forced myself to check the door locks and turn out the lights. Didn't even bother to pull on pajamas before I fell into bed and sleep.

In the middle of the night, I woke up.

Carrie's necklace!

I scrambled out of bed, and dumped my laundry basket on the floor. My jeans were still clammy wet, but the little velvet bag was safe in the pocket.

Thank you, Lord.

I set Carrie's emerald and diamond necklace on my dresser and crawled back into bed. This time I did don my jammies first.

****

I didn't get around to examining Carrie's necklace until the clinic closed and I slipped home for a late afternoon lunch.

I sat with my tuna sandwich, Carrie's beautiful necklace, and a jewelry supply catalogue spread across the table in front of me. Sheba also sat on the table waiting for loose bits to fall from my sandwich. She knew there were always some.

I'd quickly realized repairing the necklace's broken clasp—an elegant European style popular in high end pieces—was beyond my skill set. Replacing it might be my only solution. I elbowed Sheba aside, and flipped pages, looking for a duplicate clasp to order. Problem was, my catalogues didn't offer anything comparable.

I called Mr. Piteaux for advice.

"If you must know," he said in his distinctive nasal. "I originally sold the necklace to Mr. Oui, so yes, I am quite familiar with the clasp. I may have something that will help."

"If I brought it to you this afternoon?"

"This afternoon? Excellent. I'll have everything ready. If the problem is what I think, I can replace the clasp while you wait."

I hesitated. "This is rather embarrassing, but I suspect Carrie asked me to repair the clasp because she can't really afford to replace it right now. Not on top of Claude's funeral expenses." The bill for her mom's residence flashed through my mind, too. "I was hoping perhaps you could just show me?"

Mr. Piteaux cleared his throat. "Say no more. The replacement will be my gift. I've been hoping for an opportunity to express my condolences. Perhaps this will help in some small way."

I thanked Mr. Piteaux for his graciousness and prepared a to-do list for my trip into town. While at work, I remembered that I'd left the seven page checklist Carrie gave me on the beach. I called, and she emailed me a second copy. That list I divided, and printed off. Then I emailed each Steering Committee member the section of the checklist that applied to them. They were now responsible to make sure every item on their list was looked after. I would not be doing the job for them.

I got some immediate, panicked replies, but I stood firm. I was not going to usurp their responsibilities, or the credit they deserved. The 'not taking the credit' part went over so well, I decided to give each person a recognition award. They could set it on their mantle, hang it on their wall, stuff it in their bathroom closet. It didn't matter to me what they did with it, as long as they realized their hard work was appreciated.

I found a certificate template online, and printed them on parchment samples I had at home—I planned doing our wedding invitations the same way. I'd buy mats, and fancy frames for the certificates, ribbons, gift wrap and matching thank-you cards while in town. There were things on the checklist that fell under my purview. With Hum Harbour Daze only two sleeps away, I would get those items, too.

Meanwhile, I still needed to confirm whether the tent Sam found was for his purposes—did the lobster boat races need a giant tent?—or mine. I meant Reverend Innes's.

Ash was back working at Dunmaglass. Geoff was updating patient charts. I had the entire afternoon to run errands.

First, I stopped at Piteaux Jewelers and left the necklace with Mr. Piteaux. Then I power shopped through the mall, hitting a couple of other downtown stores to round out the trip.

Mr. Piteaux was waiting for me by the time I returned. His face wore a very distressed expression, and I felt my heart sink. "You couldn't fix it," I said.

"Oh no, I fixed it. It was really a very simple procedure." He spread the necklace on a black velvet cloth. The emerald and diamonds shimmered with blinding beauty. The new clasp looked perfect.

I stroked it with a cautious finger. Carrie's necklace was, without doubt, the most expensive piece of jewelry I'd ever touched. I felt honored, and way out of my class at the same time.

Mr. Piteaux continued to frown.

"Is something wrong with it?"

"I am uncomfortable asking, but you're sure this is the necklace Carrie gave you? The same one Claude purchased here?"

I yanked back my hand. "It's the one she gave me. And I know she wears it all the time." I flashed back to the moment I bumped it off her bedside table. "Except when she's sleeping. So it must be the necklace Claude gave her. She never lets anyone else near it. "

No, that wasn't true. The image of Black Hair

yanking it from her throat filled my mind. "Why do you ask?"

"As I said, I find this is quite uncomfortable, but this is not the necklace I sold Claude Oui."

How could that be? Carrie wore it everywhere. She and Claude would've known, immediately, if it wasn't the same necklace he'd given her. Wouldn't they?

"Then whose necklace is it?"

"This may still be Carrie Hunter's necklace."

"I don't understand."

He patted the piece sadly, as I imagine he'd pat a troublesome child. "This is a reproduction."

"It's fake?" I fell back a step. "Do you think she knows?"

"There's more. A gentleman came in the other day, and asked me to appraise this necklace."

"Who? What did he look like? This exact one? You're sure?"

He chuckled at my string of questions. "The man didn't give me his name, and I had no cause to demand identification because, as I told him, this is an exquisite looking piece, but the stones are man-made."

"Do you remember what he looked like?"

Mr. Piteaux fidgeted with the necklace. "Jewelry I remember, faces, not so much, I'm afraid. He wasn't from around here. Does that help?"

Not really. "Do you suppose Carrie knows the stones are fake?"

"I couldn't say."

I swallowed. Could Black Hair be this mystery man? Was he checking out Carrie's necklace when he came to see Mr. Piteaux, but changed his mind when he saw Geoff and me? Did that mean he recognized us?

"What should I do?"

"At this point, since no crime's been reported, no fraud committed, you've nothing to tell your brother." Like everyone else in these parts, he knew Andrew was a cop. "And there's always the possibility that Carrie already knows."

"She knows?"

"Haven't you wondered why she brought the broken necklace to you, not me?"

"I thought it was because she was busy and their finances were tight."

"Equally plausible reasons for committing the switch herself."

I stared at the necklace, repulsed by its counterfeit glitter. "I have to give it back to her."

"Of course." He carefully coiled the necklace, and slid it into the velvet bag I'd brought it in.

"I'll pay for the clasp myself."

"The necklace's being a reproduction is of no consequence to our little transaction. I promised to replace the clasp as my gift to Mrs. Oui. I'm a man of my word."

I opened my purse, and Mr. Piteaux dropped in the necklace bag. "Have you any advice?"

He folded the velvet display cloth in thirds and rolled it up like a scroll. "Pray?"

I did that all the way home. Then I found Geoff.

36

The breeze from the harbor gently flapped the fringe on Geoff's patio umbrella. He pinched the bridge of his nose as I spilled everything. Geoff agreed that Black Hair's aborted visit to Piteaux's now made sense. He must have known we knew Carrie, and he didn't want us seeing him with her necklace.

"Well?" I asked. "What should I do?"

"I think you need to return the necklace to Carrie."

"And say what?"

He thought for a moment. "Say that you couldn't repair the clasp yourself, so you took it to Mr. Piteaux, and he fixed it."

I felt relieved. "All true."

"You considered lying?"

"I considered keeping my mouth shut. I don't want to upset Carrie. If I tell her the necklace she loves is a fake…"

"It's her husband she loves. The necklace is just a token."

I spun my glass of iced tea, watching the ice cubes swirl in the mini-vortex I'd created. "But if he gave her a fake token, doesn't that imply his affection was fake, too?"

"Mr. Piteaux said the necklace Claude purchased was real. Therefore, the switch happened sometime in the intervening years."

"But does she need to know about it right now?

Why not let things settle down, first?"

He took a long drink from his glass. "How long do you suppose that will take?"

I tugged my ponytail. "At least until after the weekend and Hum Harbour Daze."

"So you plan to hide the truth for five days."

"Should I wait longer before telling her? What if, as Mr. Piteaux suggested, she already knows?"

"I'll admit that's an interesting theory. But, from our point of view, does it matter? If Carrie or Claude created a duplicate for her to wear in public, it was their choice. Even if they cashed in the real thing and commissioned the replica so no one would find out, that's still their prerogative. Of course, if one of them made the switch without informing the other, that'd be an awfully hurtful lie. But unless one of them made a fraudulent insurance claim, still not a crime."

"Which I don't think Carrie is doing. It's just, after seeing Black Hair rip the necklace from her throat—"

Geoff held up his hand. "You need to tell Andrew."

"We don't even know who Black Hair is."

"He's someone she knows well enough to let into her house at night."

"And hug." Considering Carrie's prickly personality, I couldn't imagine her list of huggable men was very long.

"LeClerc asked if you knew anything about her personal life."

"I don't, except for this."

"You need to tell them about the necklace, too, since it was somehow involved in their argument."

"Before or after I give it back to Carrie?"

Geoff glanced along the curve of the shore toward

Hunter Hall. "She's out in her garden with Caber. Why don't we go and see her first. Maybe simply mentioning Mr. Piteaux will spark a reaction."

Spark. A word that would take on a whole new connotation before the week was over.

****

Carrie'd abandoned gardening by the time we arrived. She was lounging on a patio chaise, sipping a slender glass of something pale, a decorative slice of lemon on the rim. Sunglasses hid her eyes. Her gardening gloves and trowel lay on the flagstone beside her chair.

"Would you like something cold?" She waved her glass as we pulled up matching patio chairs. "You know where things are, Gailynn. Help yourself."

I felt like the hired help. "Thanks, but no, we're fine. I brought back your necklace."

She sat up. "You fixed it? You're a lifesaver."

I passed her the velvet bag.

She opened the drawstring, spilled the necklace onto her palm, flicked the clasp with her fingertip. "Looks great—like new." When she put it on, the emerald glittered unnaturally bright against her skin. "I felt naked without it. I can't thank you enough." She resumed her reclining position.

"You're welcome," I said. "But it's actually Mr. Piteaux you should thank."

"Oh?" Did I imagine her smile chilled?

"I couldn't repair the clasp, and I didn't have a suitable replacement, so I called Mr. Piteaux for help. Apparently, he sold the original necklace to Claude."

She lifted her sunglasses. "The original necklace?"

"Sorry, I meant originally sold the necklace."

Her sunglasses dropped back into place.

"So he very graciously replaced the clasp free of charge."

"That was kind."

"I dropped the necklace off, ran some errands, and by the time I came back he had the clasp replaced, and the necklace cleaned."

She nodded.

"I don't suppose he could help himself. He's rather paternal about his jewelry."

"Paternal?" she repeated.

"Caring. Protective. Maybe paternal's the wrong word."

"I think it's the right choice," said Geoff.

Carrie pressed her hand over the emerald, but said nothing.

I knew Geoff thought we should tell Carrie that her necklace was a fake, but he was leaving the revelation to me. And I wasn't feeling revealing. Instead, I filled the awkward silence by talking to Caber.

"How are the Hum Harbour Daze preparations coming?" she asked eventually.

"I think they're going well. I've given everyone their section of the final checklist you gave me."

"You have to look after those things yourself, Gailynn."

I smiled. "I'm confident the different committee members can handle their own responsibilities."

"You seriously expect someone like your brother—no offence intended, but Sam is a bit lackadaisical—to care about the kind of details that need to be looked after?"

I stiffened defensively. My brother, Sam, might not rise to the Hunters' standards of what made a man successful, but he knew fishing boats and engines. What more did he need to run boat races? "Actually, I do."

"Then you'll be sadly disappointed."

"You would never have given Gai your job, if you really believed that," said Geoff.

Carrie scrutinized him over the top of her sunglasses.

"From what I hear, you've been in charge of Hum Harbour Daze since your father passed away. And his father organized the festival before him."

"Your point?"

"Putting Gai in charge was your idea. And when Hum Harbour Daze is over you can take credit for making a good decision."

She pushed her glasses back up her nose. I'm not sure she was convinced. Who knew? Maybe that was the point. When it bombed this year I would be blamed, and people would beg her to reclaim the chairmanship next year when, once again, she was better able to focus on the job.

Geoff held out his hand to me. "We're off. Gai and I have an appointment with Andrew and Inspector LeClerc."

We did?

"They wanted to talk to us about someone who's been lurking around town."

They did?

"I don't suppose you've noticed anyone you don't recognize?"

Carrie sipped her drink. Apparently not.

****

I didn't expect to meet my brother immediately, but that's exactly what Geoff had in mind. Pulling out his phone, he texted Andrew as we left Hunter Hall.

Andrew responded.

We took the shortest route to the police station—straight up Blair Street. It had been suggested Blair should be turned into a bobsled run during the winter and a mountain bike trail in summer. Personally, I thought the slope was too steep for safety.

Despite regularly walking up and down Hum Harbour's mountain-like streets, I was short of breath when we reached the police station. Jogging to keep up with Geoff's long strides might have contributed.

Andrew and LeClerc sat on opposite ends of Andrew's desk, feet propped on the desktop, eating pizza from a Hubris Heron take-out box.

Geoff helped himself to a slice without asking.

"So what's the deal?" asked Andrew.

"This is my idea," Geoff said. "Got that?"

Andrew flicked a stray pepperoni from his tie, leaving a greasy residue, and LeClerc handed him a paper napkin. "You have something for us?"

"Has anyone reported seeing a stranger hanging around town recently?"

LeClerc grinned. "Is this little village so quiet, you alert police every time a stranger passes through?"

Andrew licked the napkin and dabbed at his tie. "We're pretty much off the beaten track. People come to eat at the Heron, or a stray tourist might drop by Gai's shop, but normally, folks are in and out of town within an hour or two. Tops."

"Does that mean you know who he is?" I asked.

"Who who is?"

"Black Hair, the guy who's been around since Claude died. I saw him the first time parked outside the curling club during the Steering Committee's meeting."

LeClerc frowned. "Steering Committee?" Perhaps not a familiar term.

"I'll explain later," said Andrew. "What day was that?"

I rewound a calendar in my head. "Pretty sure it was the Thursday after Claude died, but before the memorial."

"What was this man doing that you remember him so well?" asked LeClerc. "No wait, you remember him because he was a stranger."

"Yes, there's that. But it was really his hair that caught my attention."

"What about his hair?"

"It was black."

LeClerc glanced to Andrew for clarification.

"You've met our family," said Andrew. "Gai's a might sensitive about hair color." As if the years of hurtful teasing were irrelevant.

I felt Geoff's hand on my shoulder. "Don't bait her, Andrew."

My brother looked at Geoff in surprise. The two had known each other since babyhood, and except for the years Geoff went to medical school and then Somalia, they'd been inseparable best friends. Geoff's return to Hum Harbour rekindled that friendship.

Andrew nodded his head almost imperceptibly. When next he looked at me, there was something different in his eyes, as though he was seeing me—perhaps for the very first time—as something other than an irrelevant little sister. And that that might actually be positive.

"Where else have you seen him?"

I ticked them off on my fingers. "Upstairs at Hunter Hall looking for the bathroom. That was during the reception. Piteaux Jewelers. He left when he saw Geoff and me."

"Any more?"

I glanced at Geoff.

"You need to tell them, especially in light of everything else you know."

Andrew's feet hit the floor, and he leaned closer. "What else do you know?"

"I saw Carrie and Black Hair arguing in her kitchen. I was walking on the beach—I couldn't sleep—and I happened to look up and see them. I wasn't spying. I didn't go that way with any intention of checking up on Carrie. I just looked, the lights were on in her kitchen, and I saw."

"Carrie Hunter-Oui and this man argued in her kitchen," repeated LeClerc. "You know they argued because you heard what they said?"

"I know they argued because he was waving his hands, then he grabbed her necklace and ripped it from her neck, and she started crying, and he hugged her and patted her back. Maybe, probably, she was still crying when he hugged her."

"I recall the necklace," said LeClerc. "Impressive."

Andrew asked, "Was the hug romantic? Brotherly? Reciprocated? Rebuffed?"

I replayed the scene. "I thought it looked reluctant. Like he felt obliged to hold her. He'd made her cry, but he wasn't really feeling the love, if you know what I mean."

"What happened next?"

"I didn't hang around to see."

Andrew grunted. "What else do you have for us?"

Geoff answered for me. "Carrie asked Gai to fix the broken clasp on her necklace."

"He broke the clasp when he grabbed it?"

I nodded. "I couldn't fix it, though, so I asked Mr. Piteaux."

"The jeweler again," said Andrew. The way he said again stopped me.

"Do you think he's involved?"

"Finish your story, Gai."

"He, Mr. Piteaux, replaced the clasp, but—" I glanced at Geoff. "--he said a man had brought the very same necklace in to be appraised, and it's not real. Well, the necklace is a real necklace, of course, but the stones aren't. They're fake."

LeClerc tossed the empty pizza box into the trashcan. "It's not uncommon for wealthy people to own quality copies of their pieces, to wear them instead of the real thing."

"Exactly," I agreed, referring to my comprehensive knowledge of heist movies.

"And the real necklace?" asked Geoff.

"In a safe deposit box, perhaps."

I felt my pulse quicken. "Do you think the necklace might be important?"

"There's no way of knowing. And up to this point, we have been working the theory Claude's death was connected to the missing frogs. So we had no cause to ask Carrie about a safe deposit box."

"Couldn't you manufacture a cause?"

"Your sister has an interesting mind," said LeClerc.

"Unfortunately." Andrew glanced sharply at Geoff. "I wasn't baiting her."

"Was Madame Oui aware her necklace is a reproduction?"

"I sowed some hints. Gave her a chance to respond."

"Did she?"

I looked to Geoff for his thoughts. "Do you think she took the bait?"

"Not sure."

LeClerc grabbed his jacket from the back of his chair. "Let us go, MacDonald."

My brother was on his feet, brushing off his pants, and straightening his tie.

"You two may as well come along," said LeClerc. "Unless you have plans?"

I didn't give Geoff a chance to answer. "Thank you, we'd be delighted."

Geoff held me back, otherwise I'd have beaten Andrew and LeClerc to the door. "Try to sound like it's a murder investigation, not a tea party," he whispered.

I nodded and adjusted my face. I hoped my eyes weren't shining.

37

Geoff and I were climbing into the back seat of the police cruiser when Reverend Innes puffed into the station's small parking lot. His face was redder than his MacBean tartan vest. (The reverend's mother was a MacBean.)

"What's happened?" asked Andrew.

Reverend Innes smoothed his vest as he caught his breath.

"There's been a terrible disaster."

Andrew and LeClerc shifted into emergency-mode. "What happened? Where?"

I scanned the town spreading down the hillside below us. Did I see smoke? Should we call the volunteer fire department? An ambulance?

"It's Sam," said Reverend Innes.

We stiffened—Andrew and me because Sam's our oldest brother, Geoff because his sister, Sasha, is married to Sam.

Lord, is Sam all right?

"He'd arranged for a tent for the crafters and farmer's market folks. You knew that, didn't you?"

"I'd heard, but—"

Reverend Innes shook his head emphatically. "I don't know what we would have done if he hadn't come forward."

LeClerc, cell phone out, was requesting emergency back-up from Antigonish.

"They dropped it off at the curling rink. We were planning to set it up in the parking lot—"

Enough with the tent already.

"What's wrong?" I practically shouted.

"He had a crew of guys arranged to help, because we need it up tonight."

Andrew grabbed Reverend Innes's shoulders and shook him. "Do we need emergency responders, man?"

Reverend Innes pulled back in alarm. "Oh dear me, no. Nothing like that. We need Gailynn."

"Gai?" Andrew repeated, incredulously.

"I don't know how he did it, but Sam dislocated his shoulder while he was unloading the tent. Sasha's taken him into Emergency at the hospital—sorry, Geoff, we couldn't find you at the clinic—but we still need that tent up."

LeClerc snapped his phone closed, and Andrew's shoulders sagged with what I assume was relief.

I felt equally relieved. "What do you need me for?"

Reverend Innes tugged his vest. "Well, you're the chair of the Steering Committee, and whenever we have a problem, the chair's the one who solves it."

"What's the problem?"

"Where do you want the tent?"

"Wherever the tent's supposed to go." That seemed obvious to me.

"No one knows where the tent's supposed to go."

"And I do?"

"You're the chair. You're in charge of this kind of thing."

I felt Geoff's hand on my shoulder. "Looks like you're needed somewhere else."

****

I expected to find the unloaded mega-tent and a dozen fishermen in the curling club's parking lot, waiting to set up. The tent was there all right, a ten-ton mass of canvas, poles, and rope, but there were only two men.

"Lodge night," one said. "We stayed as long as we could but, sorry, we can't be late for the meeting. We're putting the final touches on the parade float." Every year the lodge glued ten zillion red tissue paper carnations to a giant mechanical lobster that spewed bubbles from its snapping claws. It used to throw out candy until the year my grandmother got hit in the face and her glasses broke.

"What am I supposed to do?" I asked Reverend Innes. "I can't set this up by myself."

"Since they put the new blacktop down, I don't think we can set up the tent here, anyway," said Geoff.

"Then where do we put it?" I glanced up and down the street.

There was a vacant lot beyond the Bait 'n Tackle, overgrown with waist high grass and Queen Anne's Lace. Fishermen stacked their broken lobster traps at one end and burned them on Guy Fawkes Day.

Geoff said, "Why not there?"

A short block from the ball diamonds, where the midway crew was busy setting up, the vacant lot was also an easy walk to the curling club's parking area and the wharf—lobster boat central. And with a clump of trees at one side, there would even be shade, something the parking lot lacked. We strolled over to investigate.

The ground seemed flat, the space adequate to the task.

"Let's hope this'll do." I looked at Reverend Innes. "Do you have a lawn mower we can borrow?"

"Nothing that will handle this mess. You need a ride on, like Ross Murray has. Why not give him a call?"

Ross, however, was at the lodge meeting gluing carnations.

I called Dad. Within minutes, he arrived with Josh, Ash's dad, and three heavy-duty gas mowers. They spent the next two hours shearing the weeds, while Reverend Innes, Geoff, and I transported tent parts to the new site in the back of Josh's red hearse.

It was dark by the time we were ready to set up. Dad called Mom, who called several of my aunts, uncles and cousins. It was the Sunday afternoon clan gathering all over again.

Everyone parked their vehicles around the field, like circled wagons and flipped on the headlights. Tent assembly began.

I'd like to have said it went up without a hitch or that the hitches were minimal. Truth was none of us knew what we were doing. By one AM, we were exhausted, frustrated, and still staring at the mess of poles and canvas—the thing had collapsed for the third time. Yes, third.

I was close to tears. "I give up."

Dad hugged me. "Let's call it a night. Things'll look better in the morning."

I didn't believe him, but I had no energy to argue. We left everything where it was. If the frog thief, that American jewel thief, or anyone else wanted to steal the stupid tent, they could help themselves. I was too tired to care.

****

My phone rang and my doorbell buzzed.

Geoff, stuck outside in the rain, rapped loudly on the sliding glass door.

I let him in. "Tell me this is a dream, and when I wake up it'll be over?"

"The delivery folks are downstairs wanting to know where you want the crafters' tables."

"Isn't that Reverend Innes's job?"

"He sent them here because the tent's not up yet."

"It's not up because he didn't get people to set it up."

"Gai."

I hung my head. "I guess they could deliver them to where the tent will be, whenever I get it set up. Unless the rain will ruin them."

He wrapped his arms around me. "They're plastic tables."

Therefore, rain-proof?

"Tell them to give me a minute, and I'll meet them there to unload."

Out of habit, I checked my answering machine. One from Andrew. *Argh.* I did not have time for him now. I erased the message and jumped into the shower.

Half an hour later, Geoff was at work, and I was standing under an umbrella, surveying the stack of rain soaked plastic tables and the soggy canvas tent lying on the ground. "What are we supposed to do with these?"

Brother Sam stood beside me, his arm in a sling. "Doc in Emergency said I shouldn't use the arm for a few days. Give the tendons and ligaments a chance to recover." At least he was here.

"I'm asking for ideas."

He rubbed his chin with his good hand. "Well, until you get that tent up…it's supposed to stop raining sometime this morning, but that sucker's gonna be heavy as sin now that it's water-logged. Dunno whose gonna be able to lift it, even if we knew how to set it up."

"Didn't the guy you borrowed it from leave instructions?"

"It was the wife that let me into the shed to get it, so I never actually talked to him, myself."

"It's supposed to stop raining?"

Sam grunted. "Just 'cause the weatherman says it's gonna be sunny, that don't mean the sun's actually gonna shine. But you know that."

"Then what we need is for you to get hold of the guy you rented the tent from and ask him, as nicely as you can"—I could hear my voice rising—"to please come down here and show us how to set this stupid thing up!"

"You don't have to shout."

I took a deep breath. "I'm sorry."

Sam fisted and unfisted the hand of his injured arm. "I don't think I can get him."

"Why not?"

"His wife said he was leaving for Halifax this morning."

"Call, anyway. Offer to pay him."

He glared down at me. "For explaining how to set up his tent?"

"It's no good to us lying in a sodden mess in the middle of a field!"

"It wasn't me who left it out in the rain!"

My phone chirped. I whipped it out of my pocket, and without checking to see who it was, shouted, "What?"

"Aren't we a little testy this morning."

I turned my back on Sam. "Andrew, I haven't got time for this, this morning."

"I know. Dad told us about your situation."

Us? Great. Who else was going to phone and gloat?

"Look, unless you have something constructive to offer, I am up to my eyeballs right now, so I'm sorry, but I don't have time to look at your pictures."

"I'm not calling about that."

"Then why?"

"Raoul has an idea about how we can get your tent up and maybe catch a killer at the same time."

My spirit perked. "He could do that?"

"I don't know, but if you still need help getting that tent up?"

"I do!"

"Give us half an hour. We'll meet you beside the Bait 'n Tackle."

"Even if it's still raining?"

"Do you want our help or not?"

My annoyance forgotten, I smiled at Sam as I re-stowed my phone in my pocket. "Looks like the cavalry is on the way."

38

Ten a.m. Three dozen men, women, and kids, including one-armed Sam, stood around the tent in the wet mowed grass. It had stopped raining. A tiny streak of blue sky peeked through the clouds. I took that as a sign of God's blessing.

Raoul LeClerc rubbed his hands together in anticipation. He'd explained the process. We all had our jobs. So on the count of three, we were going to hoist three sides of the tent until the pooled water ran off.

One, two, three.

It weighed a ton, and I didn't mean that figuratively, but, according to Sam's shouted progress reports, it was working. Once the water'd drained into the ground we assembled tent poles. Raoul sketched a rough diagram showing us what went where. He'd apparently spent two summers in college working for a party rental company, so tents were second nature to him.

We arranged the poles around the tent and prepared the ropes and pegs. When Danny-Boy Murdock jumped out of the car, we cheered. Danny-Boy was Raoul's secret weapon. He figured any man who tossed telephone poles for fun, should be able to erect the tent's center pole no problem.

Raoul ran through the instructions one last time. "If the tent was dry this would be easy." Yeah, right.

"Wet canvas is heavier, but the job is the same. We have canvas lifters. We have pole lifters. We have tent peggers. Everyone ready?"

We all shouted, "Ready!"

"Lift!"

I slipped on the wet grass, struggled to my feet, and lifted with all my might. Danny-Boy ran from one tent pole lifter to the next, helping each straighten and stabilize their pole, while the peggers pegged the ropes. Then, like a man about to bear the weight of the world on his shoulders, he waddled, stoop-backed under the big top, and hoisted the center pole.

What a thing to behold. Danny-Boy groaning and straining under the weight of the canvas, as he raised the center pole. He lifted the massive metal mast until it was vertical.

Raoul slid a weight-bearing cement block underneath—without it, the pole would have sunk deep into the wet ground. Raoul slapped Danny-Boy on the back.

I rushed forward to give my own thanks.

"You have no idea how much I appreciate what you've done for us."

Danny-Boy's already large grin widened as others playfully punched his shoulder, pumped his arm, squeezed his hand.

"You've saved the day!" said one.

"You've saved the whole festival!" said another.

Several men hoisted Danny-Boy onto their shoulders and marched him around the tent. Ross Murray appeared beside me. "Well, Gai, looks like you came through after all."

"Thanks."

"Hey, don't thank me. I still think it was a mistake

to ditch old Danny-Boy as parade marshal. You're just lucky the man doesn't hold a grudge."

Raoul took Ross's place when he stamped off to join the hail Danny-Boy parade. "Danny Murdock does not hold a grudge?"

"That's how I'd have described Wee Claude. But Danny-Boy? If he turns out to be the killer, I'd say he's taken grudge-holding to a whole new level."

"If he is the killer."

We watched Danny-Boy soak up the adulation. "Are you going to tell me what you suspect?"

He smiled. "Not without proof."

I shook his hand. "Well, thanks for saving the tent. I know this had nothing to do with your investigation."

He winked. "Your mama bribed me with a peach pie of my very own. How could I resist?"

There were still issues to be resolved, like setting up tables, stringing lights, and directing the set-up of portable toilets. All the while the folded checklist I'd gotten from Carrie felt stiff in my back pocket. In the midst of the business, I noticed Danny-Boy being loaded into the police cruiser with Andrew and Raoul, and later, a tow truck hauled away Danny-Boy's car.

Was that how LeClerc planned to get his proof?

There was a part of me—deep down inside where I was trying to ignore it—that said no. Danny-Boy was not our man. Which was a problem, because if Danny-Boy wasn't the killer, and Josh wasn't the killer, that left the mysterious Black Hair. Whoever he was.

And if not Black Hair? I couldn't suppress the shiver, as I watched the people working around me. Was it one of them?

Sam snapped his fingers in front of my face.

"Earth to Gai?"

I pushed his hand away.

"Did you hear what I said? I need someone to help with the fireworks."

Besides overseeing the lobster boat races, Sam always launched Hum Harbour Daze opening with night fireworks from his boat. It was a magnificent show. The brilliant explosions reflected in the harbor, doubling their fiery splendor. It was, without a doubt, my favorite part of the whole weekend.

He had a point. I couldn't envision him standing on the lobster boat's roof, launching exploding rockets with one good arm, while the boat bounced and bobbed beneath his feet. Every time I tried, I saw him pitching head first into the sea.

I studied my brother thoughtfully. Sam wasn't the kind of man who gave in easily. If he was requesting help, it meant he really needed help. "Is one person going to be enough?"

"It's not hard work, Gai. Even you could do what needs to be done."

"Me?" I laughed. "On a boat?"

"OK, not you, but anyone with sea legs. All they need are two hands, and a good sense of balance."

"Do you care how old he is?"

"As long as he can follow directions. Got someone in mind?"

"Maybe."

I was thinking of Josh, and I knew where I'd find him. At Dunmaglass, of course.

****

As I rounded the corner onto Main Street, I

spotted a man standing on the sidewalk across from Dunmaglass. He seemed to be watching the Hubris Heron—Geoff's upstairs windows, actually—as he slowly smoked a cigarette. Despite the ball cap pulled low over his eyes, I recognized him immediately. Black Hair.

I ducked back behind the corner, flattened myself against the wall. Why was he watching Geoff's apartment? What should I do? Walk up and say hi? For whatever reason, he turned tail and ran the moment he saw Geoff and me at the jewelers. What were the chances he'd stick around long enough to talk to me?

I peeked again; he was still there. I pulled out my cell phone.

Ash picked up after one ring, and I cut through her pleasant 'good morning, Dunmaglass' spiel. "Is Josh with you?"

"Gai?"

Peering around the building, I said, "Listen, and don't interrupt. See that guy across the street?"

Silence.

"Ash, did you hear me?"

"You said not to interrupt."

"You can still answer!"

"Then, yeah, I see him."

"Get Josh to go talk to him."

"How do you know Josh is here?"

"He can talk about anything. I don't care. But get him to find out the guy's name."

"That's something, not anything."

"Ash! He's leaving!"

"What do you want Josh to do? Follow the guy?" She said it like it was a joke.

"Yes! Follow him, and find out who he is, and

where he goes."

"Seriously?"

"Ash, hurry! The guy's about to disappear."

A second later Josh flew out the door, ran half a block, and braked before shifting to a nonchalant pace. In a moment, he and Black Hair were around the corner and out of sight.

Should I interrupt Andrew and tell him what was afoot?

The dispatcher answered my call.

"I'm assuming Andrew and Raoul, ah, Inspector LeClerc, are interviewing Danny-Boy. You don't have to answer that, Rose, but could you take them this message, please?" I paused, imagining her grabbing the pink message pad and a pen. "Black-haired man spotted outside Dunmaglass. Josh Pry in pursuit."

"Do you want to wait for an answer?"

"I'm pretty sure I know what it would be." I could almost see her move to disconnect. "Wait! Tell Andrew to call me back if we should discontinue the tail. OK? And wait! Tell him I'm checking Dunmaglass's video surveillance. I may have the guy's picture."

"The black-haired man?"

"Yeah. Got all that?"

"Ten-four."

My fancy surveillance system had failed me when the rock throwers broke the shop's window because the vandals had stayed beyond the camera's range. Hopefully, their newly adjusted angle would be enough to catch Black-Hair posing on the sidewalk. Without stopping to greet Ash, I dashed straight through the shop and upstairs to my spare room/office. The security system was set up so that, with the click of my mouse, I could watch the pictures stored on a special computer. I pulled up a chair, switched on the monitor, and hit rewind—which I knew wasn't the appropriate techie terminology. Sheba made herself at home on my lap.

I didn't have to go back very far. With time stamped snaps taken every ten seconds, several showed the back of his head, two of his profile, and one blurred shot of his face, probably as he was turning to leave. Considering the price I'd paid for this system, they could have installed a camera with a better shutter speed. I'd talk to the company about that.

I printed 8x10 copies of each snap, and tucked them into a folder. Since there was still no word from Andrew, or LeClerc—busy interrogating Danny-Boy, no doubt—I decided to deliver the pictures to the police station myself.

Ash waylaid me, cell phone to her ear. "Josh's followed the guy to the curling rink. He's sitting in his pickup drinking a can of pop. What do you want Josh to do?"

"Wander over and say hi, maybe? If they're at the curling rink, there's lots of stuff going on. Tell Josh to get him talking so we can find out the guy's name."

Ash relayed my instructions.

"What's his license plate?" I scribbled it on the folder, another bit of the puzzle for Andrew and LeClerc.

Just in case, I also grabbed a plastic bag from under the counter—the kind with a zip. I sometimes used them when I packaged earrings. As I hoped, I found the discarded cigarette butt where Black Hair had been standing. I popped it into the bag. Now we had Black Hair's DNA.

****

I wasn't sure Andrew and LeClerc were as impressed with my initiative as I'd expected. I waved at Andrew, who glared at me through the open door of his office.

Danny-Boy, his back to me, occupied the chair facing Andrew's desk.

LeClerc sat behind Andrew's desk, and my brother half-perched on the desk's corner.

"What's it been, a half-hour?" I asked Rose.

"You know you'll get me in trouble with the boss if I answer that."

I had a somewhat deserved reputation for interfering, and Andrew'd warned everyone who worked at the police station that I was not, under any circumstances, allowed beyond the entrance.

I rested my elbows on the counter. "Well, I wouldn't be me if I didn't ask."

"Where's that man of yours?"

"Geoff?" I hadn't seen him or thought of him in—I checked my watch—one hour and thirty-four minutes. "He's helping me with Hum Harbour Daze."

"The guys giving you a hard time?"

"How did you know?"

She smiled benevolently. "Honey, your heart was in the right place when you offered to help Carrie Hunter out this year…"

"But?"

"It's a job that needs a stronger hand."

"What's wrong with my hands?"

She reached across and squeezed one. "Not a thing. I'm just glad that man of yours is lending you his."

I pulled the checklist out of my back pocket.

Geoff had taken responsibility for a couple of the pages. Well, actually, the committee members were still responsible, but he was surreptitiously confirming that they were indeed doing the things required. Geoff was better at surreptitious than I was. I headed back to the curling club, Hum Harbour Daze central, to see how other activities were developing.

39

Sam, his left arm still in the sling, was awkwardly assembling the sign-in booth for the lobster boat races. I started toward him, knowing my help was better than no help, and remembered another job he might appreciate more. Finding him a helper for the fireworks.

Josh leaned against the curling club's wall, sucking lime green slushy up a straw, as he ogled a cluster of giggling girls. Their uber-tight shorts drew more eyes than his.

Black Hair and his pickup were nowhere to be seen.

I shouted Josh's name several times before getting his attention and waved him over.

"You just missed him," Josh said.

"What did you find out?"

Geoff sneaked up behind me and covered my eyes. I knew it was him, of course. I always knew when Geoff was near. But I played along, feeling his hands, making ridiculous guesses like, "Brad, is that you?" Meaning Brad Pitt.

He ignored that. "What are you two up to?"

"Gai had me follow some guy to find out his name."

"What guy? What name?"

"Black Hair. He was watching your apartment."

Geoff's eyes became distant. "My place? You're

sure? Why would he do that?"

I didn't know, and I didn't like it. "I caught him on Dunmaglass's security. Dropped his picture and his cigarette butt at the police station. Josh got his license number. I gave them that, too. The rest is up to Andrew and LeClerc."

"You're determined to find out who he is."

"He's suspicious. Creeping around, watching people—what if he's who I saw watching Hunter Hall during the storm? What if he's Claude's killer?"

"Slow down."

I couldn't. I was on a roll. "We know Josh didn't do it. I have the sinking feeling Danny-Boy isn't guilty, either. Which means Claude's killer is still at large. And there is no denying Black Hair is mighty suspicious."

Geoff shook his head when I said the sinking feeling. He was not happy with my attitude. "So Black Hair's your next candidate?"

"Doesn't it scare you that he's watching people?" I glanced around making sure no one else was close enough to hear. "I think I may know who he is."

"Who?" asked Josh.

"The jewel thief they keeping talking about in the news."

When Geoff pinched the bridge of his nose like that, I knew he was trying to give me the benefit of the doubt. And not laugh. "In Hum Harbour?"

"What better place to lay low? He decided to attend Claude's funeral because there wasn't much else to do, and while he was there, he spotted Carrie's necklace."

"Claude was already dead by then. Kind of late to murder him, don't you think?"

"OK Mr. Wise-Guy, when do you think he stole Carrie's necklace?"

"Someone stole Carrie's fancy necklace?" Josh interrupted.

Geoff said, "Apart from a minor detail like, a jewel thief wouldn't need Mr. Piteaux to appraise Carrie's necklace, who would ever come to Hum Harbour if they weren't related to someone here?"

"But if he was here lying low and just happened to see Carrie and her necklace?"

He looked at me.

"He could've sneaked into Hunter Hall to steal it, but Claude caught him, so he clobbered Claude with the closest thing on hand, Carrie's frog candlestick."

"Then he hung around town long enough to switch her necklace with a duplicate he had made. No wait, he had to've had the duplicate on hand when he broke in, otherwise she'd have alerted police that it was missing, too."

I flipped my ponytail over my shoulder.

"Then he went into her house again and confronted her with his crime, ripping the fake necklace from her neck."

"You've made your point," I said testily. "If Black Hair swapped Carrie's real necklace with a fake he'd never have hung around."

Josh noisily drained his slushie. "What if he broke into Hunter Hall planning to steal the real one, but when he saw it was fake he, like, hung around, for a second chance to search the house." He tossed his empty into a nearby trash can. "Wait a minute. Did you say it's fake?"

"Except, he searched the house during Claude's reception. He still didn't find the real one, and that's why he came back a third time and argued with Carrie."

"What about Claude?"

"It was like I said, Claude caught him the first time he broke in, so he bonked Claude, never thinking he'd killed him, and escaped to try again."

"It fits," said Josh.

Geoff shook his head. "I don't believe this."

"It makes perfect sense—except for why he was watching you. We need to talk to Andrew about that."

"No," Geoff said.

"If Claude's killer is spying on you—"

"You're way off base, Gai. Give it a rest." The warning in his eyes silenced any further argument.

I turned my back on Geoff, who obviously did not appreciate my genius, and changed the subject. "Josh, how would you like to help Sam with the fireworks tomorrow night?"

"Are you, like, serious?"

"I'm always, like, serious."

"Like," said Geoff, "a word used to introduce a simile, the comparison to two different things."

I said to Josh, "There's Sam. Run over and see what he needs you to do."

Geoff dropped his arm around my shoulders. "One of these days people are going to believe you mean the outrageous things you say."

"You don't?"

"Believe that guy you call Black Hair is a murderer and jewel thief? Not in the slightest."

40

I stomped off. How could Geoff give my theories such little credence? Someone had killed Claude. Someone had stolen Carrie's necklace. Why not Black Hair? He was suspicious; no one could deny that.

People were everywhere. News of the mega-tent had spread, and it seemed like half of Hum Harbour had come to see it. I pulled out my job list, letting folks bump and jostle me as I checked for what to do next. It was hard to concentrate and not just because of the crowd. My discussion with Geoff was still running through my mind. Had I missed the mark in this murder investigation?

I stuffed my list back into my jeans pocket. No. It had to be Black Hair. There was no one else to suspect. By now, Andrew should know who he was. I turned, ready to hunt down my brother and demand to know what he'd uncovered, and walked right into Danny-Boy Murdock. He was free. His deodorant had died, and by his thin-lipped scowl, I could tell he wasn't happy.

"I suppose I have you to thank for that?"

I tried backing out of whiff range. "For what?"

He wrapped his beefy fingers around my upper arm and hauled me behind the Bait 'n Tackle. Behind the Bait 'n Tackle stank of dead fish, which was even worse than eau de Danny-Boy.

I tried shaking off his hand. "You have no right to

manhandle me!"

"Afraid I'll do to you what I did to Claude?"

"You wouldn't hit a woman. Would you?"

He released me. "Because of you, half this town wants to crown me king, and the other half vilifies me."

"I've got nothing to do with either."

"Sure you do. Think I don't know that little tent raising gimmick was your idea?"

"It wasn't."

"Or telling your brother and that RCMP guy how I went back to Claude's house that night, to get him to stick up for me with Highland Breweries."

"I never."

"Then who did?"

I held up my hands to show my innocence.

"You need to learn how to mind your own business and leave well enough alone."

"Claude Oui is dead. How is that well enough?" I demanded.

"For one, now Carrie's free of Claude the fraud."

"What do you mean, Claude the fraud?"

"It's like I told your brother and that RCMP guy. Everyone thinks Claude was some born-again hero. Teaching Sunday school. Visiting old ladies. Giving away his money. Moving to Africa to save orphans. None of it was for real."

An angry horsefly buzzed around my ears. "You think he was pretending?"

"You better believe it. He was an alky. And I told your brother and that RCMP guy so it's on record."

"Claude didn't drink."

"Not in front of people. But when I went back that second time, he could hardly stand up straight.

Staggering, slurring his words. Couldn't even handle the lights in the hallway. Had them all turned off, but one."

"He wasn't drinking, you idiot. He had a medical condition. He was staggering because some moron knocked him down earlier in the evening; the same moron who hit him with a flying hammer!"

"That was an accident. How many times do I have to tell people I didn't mean to hit anyone with that hammer!" The horsefly landed on his forearm.

"But you did punch him that night."

He smashed the fly and flicked away the bits of debris. "I never said I was a saint."

"That punch you gave Claude, on top of the flying hammer hit, makes you the number one suspect—until the coroner says otherwise."

He puffed out his chest. "If I'd killed Claude Oui don't you think your brother'd be dragging me off in chains right about now?"

I tried analyzing Claude's murder the way Andrew might.

Claude died because someone hit him in the head with a frog candlestick. Danny-Boy's punch might have left him susceptible to that fatal blow, but since Danny-Boy used his fist, not the candlestick…

"So what did you want to talk to me about?"

From a distance, a couple of people shouted something at Danny-Boy. He let out a deep breath, waved, and shouted something back. It only took a moment, but the exchange seemed enough to defuse Danny-Boy's temper.

"I wanted to say thanks for the tent thing this morning." His words were stilted, but the sentiment sounded surprisingly sincere. "Despite our differences, that was a stand up thing you did, giving me the chance to help out."

His thanks knocked me off guard. I managed an, "Oh?"

"Someone took a picture on their phone—me lifting the tent's center pole—and posted it online."

"Really?"

"I got a call from some guy at Highland Breweries. They want to talk to me. Maybe they're going to reconsider the endorsement."

What could I say? "Congratulations."

Danny-Boy lifted me off my feet in a bone crushing embrace. "I don't care what other people say, Gai, you're my kinda girl."

Geoff materialized at the perfect moment and tapped Danny-Boy's shoulder. He released me.

Fortunately, Geoff caught me before I hit the ground. "Just as long as we're clear: she might be your kind of girl, but she is, in fact, my girl. And I don't share."

Danny-Boy whacked Geoff's back, a blow so powerful it radiated through Geoff and rattled my teeth. "Good one! But thanks, I like my women bigger, stronger, and quieter."

"Then I guess Gai really isn't your type."

Danny-Boy winked at me. "But if she ever decides to turn you down, I could adapt."

I regarded him darkly. I disliked men who changed their affections more often than they changed their socks. "I thought you were in love with Carrie Hunter?"

Danny-Boy threw back his head and bellowed with laughter. He was still laughing when, ten minutes later, he climbed into the passenger seat of Ross

Murray's pickup, and they drove away.

****

Geoff and I walked to the ball field at the end of Main Street. The midway always set up there. Every year the local ball association complained about the arrangement. Midway patrons trampled the grass to death, and if it happened to rain during Hum Harbour Daze, the mucky fields were ruined for the rest of the season. But there was nowhere else big enough and flat enough to accommodate the midway.

If the midway was going to open on time, the rides had to be ready for the next day's safety inspection. So the crew was busy unloading and assembling brightly painted bumper cars, merry-go-round ponies, spinning tea cups, and, of course, the Ferris wheel. Everyone's favorite. If you were lucky enough to stop at the top of the wheel's circle, you could see every roof in town. And on a windy day, the ride took on a whole new dimension.

"What if Black Hair is actually one of the midway's front men?" asked Geoff, proving I wasn't the only one who couldn't get murder off of their mind.

"A front man?"

"Someone who goes in ahead of the midway to make sure everything's ready for their arrival."

"Then wouldn't I have heard from him?"

"If he's used to dealing with Carrie, she might've decided it was easier to look after the arrangements herself than to explain everything to you, since you don't plan to stay on as Hum Harbour Daze's chair."

"By this time next year, I'll be much too busy managing a husband and a home to be involved with

Hum Harbour Daze."

Geoff bent for a quick kiss. "Managing your husband, you say?"

I returned it, not caring what the midway folk thought.

"If you're right and Black Hair is part of the midway, he should be here. Somewhere," I said when I could breathe again. "But I don't see him. Do you?"

I saw plenty of muscle-bound guys with long hair and tattoos working up a sweat in the sun, but Black Hair was nowhere.

"Maybe, if we showed his picture around?"

"I think we're too late." Geoff pointed to my brother, who was moving from one cluster of workers to the next, flashing what I assumed was the picture I'd downloaded. By the way the carni-men kept shaking their heads, it looked like Black Hair was a total stranger.

Andrew approached us last of all. "The inspector wanted me to check with these guys, to see if they recognized Gai's mystery man."

"Did you really expect they would?" I asked.

Geoff smiled down at me. "She thinks he's the jewel thief who's been on the news lately."

Andrew snorted. "Seriously?"

"Have you got a better idea?"

"I sure don't have a worse one." Andrew held up his hands.

"I admit my theory has a few flaws—"

"You think?"

"But until we can find Black Hair and question him about his involvement with Carrie, and why he switched out her necklace, and why he's spying on Geoff, I don't see how we can eliminate him from the suspect pool."

"We? Spying on you?"

Geoff didn't look as concerned as he should. "She caught the guy staring at the Hubris Heron. "

"Not the Heron. Your apartment above the Heron."

Andrew made a time-out T with his hands. "This guy was watching Geoff's place? I thought your security camera caught him casually walking by your shop."

"Gai's afraid the guy's escalating from jewel thief to mass murderer."

"Stop talking about me like I'm not here. And I never said that."

"But you're worried," said Geoff.

"I love you. Of course, I'm worried. And I expect Andrew to keep you safe until they prove one way or the other who Black Hair is."

"If there's any credence to your cockamamie theories, and the guy is the killer, you put yourself, and anyone you con into your little scheme,"—he was looking at Geoff—"in harm's way."

"Like Josh?" said Geoff.

"You got Josh Pry involved?" Andrew's face was changing from red to purple.

I twisted my ponytail around my hand. "Can we change the subject?"

Andrew sighed. "What do you want to know?"

"What makes you think—?"

"Because you don't give up that easily. You just come at it from different directions until you get what you want. So spit it out. What do you want?"

"Well,"--I swept my hair over my squared shoulder-- "I was wondering where you found the murder weapon and if you've identified any fingerprints on it. Besides the expected ones."

He pursed his lips as he considered the ramifications of answering.

Geoff and I exchanged a meaningful look. Andrew was actually considering this?

41

"You know I can't tell you anything that might endanger the investigation," Andrew said. "But I don't think this will. We found it buried in Carrie's garden. She'd been transplanting her flowers, and I guess the killer saw an easy way to dispose of the candlestick. He hid it under her plants."

I pondered the logic in that. "And fingerprints?"

"Only Carrie's and Claude's. The killer must have worn gloves."

"As any self-respecting jewel thief would," I said.

Andrew groaned in exasperation. "Can't you do something with her?" he asked Geoff. "I tell you, the sooner you marry this woman and knock some sense into her scrambled brain—"

"Knock sense?" I felt my blood pressure soaring. "Scrambled brain?"

Andrew stared at Geoff. "This is your idea of a life partner?" Again, he threw his hands in the air. "I'm outta here."

****

I felt Geoff watching me, probably concerned about how I'd react to Andrew's criticism. I chose to elevate myself above my normal reactionary reaction, and said instead, "Obviously Black Hair's not the midway's front man, or the guys here would have recognized him."

"That doesn't make him an international jewel thief."

"But if he was just a regular guy, shouldn't Andrew have been able to trace his license number? Do you think he stole his truck, too?"

Geoff caught my hand and started walking. Attached as we were, I was forced to trot along beside him.

"He'll find Black Hair's name."

"And in the meantime?"

"Don't you have things that need doing?" He pulled out the list Carrie'd made. "I could use some help checking on everyone."

"The point of the list was so we wouldn't have to check."

"And it was a good idea. I'm just not sure it's works."

****

By 7:30 Thursday night, we had achieved the miraculous state of being ready—almost. The carnival rides and midway attractions awaited inspection. The farmers' market/crafters' tent was ready for vendors. The main stage looked splendid with its fresh coat of paint. Over the winter, some kids had vandalized the shed where it was stored and spray painted the thing with purple and green profanities. Despite my passion for all things purple, I recognized this wasn't an acceptable quality for a stage. It took six gallons of black paint to eliminate all trace of cuss words. Hopefully, it would dry by morning.

The Hum Harbour Daze parade route was

adorned with silkscreened banners on every second lamp post. The parade judges' grandstand, an elevated platform erected in front of Hum Harbour Hardware, had a newly-installed spindle railing to keep the judges and local radio personalities, from tumbling into the crowd if they became overwhelmed with enthusiasm. This had never happened, but there was always a chance the floats and marching pipe bands could inspire delirium.

The Lobster Boat Race Headquarters hut, with this year's newly-designed sign, looked great. The new trophy would stay in Dunmaglass's front window until it was time for the presentation. There was no way we were risking anything happening to the spectacular glass sculpture.

The only thing left to do, as far as I knew, was Sam's dry run. He wanted Josh to set off a couple of fireworks to make sure the two of them knew how to work together. Seemed like a sensible idea to me, too.

The sun had dipped behind the hills, so the worst of the day's heat was gone. From our vantage point on Geoff's deck, we watched assorted comings and goings. Neither of us had seen or heard from Andrew for hours. We had no idea where the murder investigation stood.

"Do you suppose Carrie'll make an appearance—double check that we've done all we're supposed to do before tomorrow?" We sat side-by-side in his lawn chairs, feet on the deck rail, eating take-out.

Geoff bit into his hamburger before answering. "I wouldn't be surprised if she locked her doors, pulled the curtains, and didn't resurface until after the whole thing was over."

I dragged an ooy-gooey fry from my poutine.

"Yeah. I'm just not sure how healthy that'd be."

Geoff quirked his eyebrow. Apparently poutine—French fries smothered in gravy and cheese curds—and discussions of health, didn't fit together in his mind.

I could see Hunter Hall from where I sat. It looked dark and still, but I was pretty sure I could identify the man walking along the beach in front of the hall. I pointed. "Isn't that–?"

Geoff leaned forward. "Black Hair? I have no idea."

"Then why did you say it was Black Hair?"

"I just guessed that's who you thought it was."

The man on the beach was getting closer.

"Well, is it?"

Geoff took another bite. "Maybe."

I set my unfinished poutine on the table. "Then let's go talk to him."

"Gai, we can't go around confronting random people just because you think..."

I didn't hear the end. I was already down the stairs, and jogging toward the shore. Tide was high, leaving a thin strip of beach. It was easy to block the man's path. Harder to know what to do next.

I opted for the *friendly maritimer* approach, held out my hand, and introduced myself. "New in these parts?"

He took a long draw from the cigarette between his tobacco-stained thumb and index finger. "I've been around."

I tried blinding him with my most irresistible smile. "I'm sorry. I didn't catch your name."

He flicked the cigarette stub into the water "I didn't give it."

I smiled all the brighter. "Have we met before? Were you at Claude Oui's funeral, maybe?"

"It was a memorial service, not a funeral."

"Yes, well—"

Black Hair's features were stone-like. If ever a man looked capable of murder. "Even in death, he denies his family." He ground out the words in guttural tones.

Gravel crunched as Geoff jogged up behind me.

Black Hair nodded, acknowledging his arrival. "I've been looking for you," he said. The more he spoke, the more I noted his accent. A lot like Inspector LeClerc's, except his French intonations were more familiar.

Geoff extended his hand around me. "Geoff Grant. Local doctor. Your brother's friend."

Brother's friend? I looked at Geoff.

"How did you know me?" asked Black Hair.

"It's not hard," said Geoff. "You and Claude look a lot alike, actually. And you sound the same."

They did? I studied Black Hair more closely. He and Claude did share the same shaped eyes, though Claude's were perpetually filled with laughter, not suspicion. And their noses? Claude's had been broken a few times, but there was a certain resemblance. "You're Claude's brother?"

"One brother. Edouard."

Geoff smiled at him. "I'm glad you were able to come. I wish you'd identified yourself at the service. Claude was loved around here. People would've wanted to talk to you. Offer their condolences."

"I did not come to Hum Harbour for sympathy."

I felt my pulse quicken. "Then why did you come?"

"Because my brother sent for me."

Geoff's brows furrowed in a puzzled V. "I'm surprised he didn't mention you were coming to me."

Black Hair—Edouard—dug the toe of his work boot into the beach stones. "I was angry. I did not want to see him. Then I did, but I came too late."

"So you weren't here the night Claude died?" I thought I asked it innocently.

Geoff apparently felt otherwise, because he stepped on my toe. Hard.

Edouard's nostrils flared. I'd seen Claude do that when he was perturbed. "Like the police, you think I could murder my own brother?" Edouard asked.

So, Andrew'd already spoken with him. "Is that what they said?"

"I have proof I was at home. Here." He pulled out his cell phone, and showed us a time-stamped photo of Edouard standing behind a dark-haired girl as she blew out her birthday candles. "My daughter, Chantelle."

I counted eight candles. "She's lovely."

"She has cerebral palsy."

I handed back the phone. Since Sam and Sasha had adopted Mara, with all of her special needs, I'd become familiar with the extra burdens and strains provincial heath care didn't always address. "That must be hard."

"Especially for my wife."

Geoff placed a reassuring hand on Edouard's shoulder.

Edoaurd didn't shrug it off. "Somehow, Claude heard about us and contacted me. He wanted to help us, he said. I said we did not need his help. It was a lie. He understood. And in the end, I came with my hat in my hand. But he was already dead."

The pain in his voice was unmistakable. I blinked

back tears. "Won't Carrie help?"

He spat on the ground. "She lives in a mansion and says she has nothing."

A few hundred feet away, Hunter Hall was smothered in gloom, still no lights on. I could understand Edouard's frustration. From the outside, it did look like Carrie was swimming in wealth.

"Is that why you argued with her?"

His nostrils flared again. "I should have gone straight home when she refused to help us. But what do I say to Chantelle? To Mary? How do I say there's no miracle to help us?" Edouard shielded a disposable lighter with his cupped hands as he lit another cigarette.

Obviously this man was not the international jewel thief I'd imagined. Jewel thieves didn't beg rich relatives for help. And since he wasn't locked up somewhere, Andrew must have confirmed Edouard's alibi for the time of Claude's murder.

Once again, I was wrong. I tried not to look too crestfallen. "Where've you been staying?"

Edouard seemed surprised by my question. "I sleep in my truck."

"And have you eaten?" asked Geoff.

"Not hungry."

He patted Edouard's shoulder—he's a very touchy person, my Geoff. "Come on. We'll feed you, anyway. And tonight you're sleeping on my futon. No more cramped pickup."

The two of them headed out, and I followed with shorter strides. I watched the way Geoff leaned close, listening attentively. If I knew my Geoff, which I did, he was already figuring out ways to help Edouard's family.

I picked up a piece of green sea glass and tucked it into my jeans pocket. Waves lapped the shore in a steady rhythm. It'd soon be dark. Sam's boat pulled away from the wharf. I watched it drone its way to the middle of the harbor and lay anchor. The running lights switched off, leaving the bobbing lobster boat almost invisible. Sam and Josh had flashlights, though, ethereal little dots of lights that seemed to dance in midair. Less ethereal were Sam's shouted orders.

Years ago, Sam had created this brace kind-of apparatus that he bolted to the boat cabin's roof. It ensured the rockets were aimed in the right direction while he lit the fuses.

Silhouetted in Sam's flashlight beam, I could see Josh on the cabin roof. He teetered and knelt, presumably maneuvering the fireworks into place for launch.

"OK, light it. Light it!" Sam's voice carried across the water.

"What's going on?" Carrie Hunter's question made me jump.

I was so fixed on Sam, Josh, and the boat that I hadn't noticed her creeping up in the darkness.

"Trial run," I explained. "Josh Pry's helping Sam with the fireworks this year, and they're working out the kinks in their system."

I could make out her pursed-lipped frown.

"Is there a problem?" I asked.

"Josh Pry's not the most reliable boy, now is he?" she said. "I know your brother's convinced he had nothing to do with Claude's death, but he did steal from my home."

"And he returned everything."

"Except my candlestick."

"You mean the murder weapon?"

Josh lit the fuse, and, like a damp sparkler, it fizzled into nothing.

"Light it again," shouted Sam. His voice sounded further away. Maybe the boat was rotating. I couldn't really see.

"Yes, the murder weapon!" said Carrie.

"That's because it wasn't with the frogs Josh took. The real killer buried it."

Spark.

"That's it!" shouted Sam. The fuse must have caught.

"Buried it where?" asked Carrie.

The tell-tale whine filled the night as the rocket shot skyward. I tried to track it. "Buried what?"

"My candlestick! The murder weapon! What do you think we're talking about?"

High above the harbor the rocket exploded into a red fireball of shimmering light. It sprayed scarlet stars across the sky, their splendid reflection mirrored in the water. The ones that fell to earth sizzled like bacon on a skillet.

I clapped—couldn't help myself.

Sam and Josh hooted in delight.

"Now we'll try the double," shouted Sam. He usually shot two rockets at a time—with fuses of varied lengths—so the display was almost constant.

"Like, for real?" Josh sounded thrilled at the prospect.

"I think they're doing well," I said. "Remember how long it took Sam to get the hang of it when he first started doing the fireworks?"

"I don't care about fireworks," said Carrie. "I care about who killed my husband!"

I stared out at the dark harbor, watching for the next rocket flares.

"Well, it wasn't Josh Pry, or Danny-Boy, or your brother-in-law, Edouard. Frankly, I've run out of suspects."

In all honesty, I couldn't be sure exactly what happened next—I mean it all happened so fast. There was crashing and splashing and shouting and swearing. The whine of dual-fired rockets and their flash as they shot across the surface of the water.

Straight at us.

42

I shoved Carrie down and landed heavily on top of her. The rockets' explosion sounded like it was right above us.

Carrie heaved me off and rose to her knees.

I stumbled to my feet. My ears rang, and I felt off balance, as though I was listing to port.

To our left, people were waving their arms and running behind the Bait 'n Tackle. Judging by the rising glow, the old lobster traps stacked up for the Guy Fawkes bonfire were ablaze.

"Get the fire department!" I didn't know if anyone heard me shouting.

I know Carrie wasn't paying attention. Slack-jawed, she stared at Hunter Hall.

I turned.

While one rocket had ignited the Bait 'n Tackle fire, the second had crashed just behind her house. Carrie's compost pile was on fire.

She took off running; I followed as fast as my shorter legs would go.

We both knew Hum Harbour's volunteer fire department was small. There was no way they could deal with the Bait 'n Tackle's fire, which potentially threatened downtown Hum Harbour, and Carrie's, as well.

By the time I reached her yard, she'd already vaulted her retaining wall and sprinted across the lawn. She emerged from the darkness dragging her garden hose and a rake.

Carrie's compost wasn't as dry as old lobster traps, more smoke than flame, but the fire had already spread to nearby bushes. Hunter Hall was the last house on the street. It backed onto brush. If that caught, the whole hillside could go up.

The warbling siren confirmed the fire truck raced to the Bait 'n Tackle, leaving us on our own.

While Carrie hosed down the bushes, I made an emergency call to Geoff on my cell. Then I grabbed the rake.

The compost smoke made it hard to work. My eyes burned as I shoveled and flipped the decaying garden weeds. I kept to the task, even after Geoff and Edouard appeared, grabbed an ax and shears from Carrie's garden shed, and hacked the adjoining brush before it caught fire, too.

In time, I recognized Andrew's voice, LeClerc, Josh and Sam. Even with one arm, Sam was stronger than most men with two. He dragged dead limbs out of the way.

We killed it. Every last smoldering bit of brush and garden debris, extinguished. As we stood, exultant, wet, black and exhausted, and surveyed the devastation of Carrie's once beautiful garden, a giggle bubbled in my throat. Hysteria, no doubt, but I couldn't quell it. It spread faster than the now-dead flames. In a moment, we were all laughing.

Carrie's laughter didn't last long.

She spotted Josh among our ranks and zeroed in.

None of us noticed her shovel.

"This is your fault!" Her voice was hoarse; we were all hoarse from breathing in the smoke.

"I didn't mean to," Josh choked on his words.

Standing beside him, Sam laid his one good hand on Josh. "I shoulda been paying closer attention, kid. I just never thought."

"Well, you should have thought!"

The flashing lights from the other end of town, reflected in the smoke-filled sky, and Carrie's garden throbbed with the alternating light and shadow. Against that strobing backdrop, her soot-covered body, even her hair bristled with pent up emotion.

"Look what you've done!" she accused.

Sam, by contrast, was a solid, immovable wall. "Now just a minute, here. It was an accident. The kid never meant for anything to catch fire."

"The kid never meant? Is that what I'm supposed to tell Claude?"

"Claude?" I looked at her closely. Were her eyes even focusing? "What's this got to do with Claude?"

She pointed a wavering finger at Josh. "I was going to let this kid off the hook for burgling my home because it was just a matter of time until police realized he'd killed my Claude."

Josh's mouth dropped open. "No, I never!"

"Just a matter of time until police found the candlestick he used to kill my husband."

Josh dragged his arm across his face. "I never!"

"And buried it under my daylilies."

He slipped out from under Sam's hand, backing away from Carrie. "You're lying! Andrew and that inspector know I had nothin' to do with Claude dying."

"And now you've tried to burn down Hunter Hall!" Carrie swung the shovel.

Metal connected with Josh's skull—a resounding

clunk. He lunged sideways and crumpled.

She raised the shovel again.

Being the closest person, I jumped on her back, wrapped my arms around her upper body, and hung on tight.

"Argh!" She sounded like the Hulk, when his eyes bugged out and his muscles bulged before he burst into that giant green monster.

I hung on to her as tight as a limpet to a stone. Digging my knees into her ribs, strengthening my grip around her arms, I screamed my loudest, "Geooooff!"

Carrie flipped me onto the ground. Her weight on top of me *whooshed* the air out of my lungs. Before the world went black, I managed to wrap my legs around her waist and wheeze one last, "Geoff."

43

"Gai?" Geoff brushed my hair from my face. "Are you OK?"

I relaxed against his shoulder. Josh, Sam, Andrew, LeClerc—Raoul—Edouard, and Carrie, stared down at us. Carrie, I noted, stood with hands behind her back, as if she were handcuffed.

I wiggled my nose and toes to see if everything worked. "Seem OK. Have I been out long?"

Andrew checked his watch. "Half a minute, give or take."

I sat up. The world tipped a bit, and then righted itself. I stood. "What did I miss?"

Carrie shook herself, maybe hoping she'd shake off the cuffs. "This is outrageous! Josh Pry kills my husband, and practically burns down the town, and I get arrested?!"

Josh sputtered, "I never killed—"

LeClerc placed his hand on Josh's shoulder. "We know, kid. We know."

"Then why does she keep saying I did?" His smoke-rasped voice cracked with indignation.

Andrew gave Carrie a gentle tug. "Let's go."

I grabbed at her cuffed hand. "Wait. I need to know something."

They stopped, and I scooted in front of them.

"How did you know the candlestick was buried under your daylilies?"

"I didn't." Carrie tried stepping around me, but Andrew held her firm.

"I heard you," I said. "So did everyone else. You accused Josh of burying the candlestick under your daylilies."

"Then I must have seen the inspector dig it out."

"No," said Geoff. He sounded thoughtful. "You were in Antigonish visiting your mother when Andrew and Inspector LeClerc uncovered the murder weapon."

"I couldn't have been. You have it wrong."

Geoff shook his head. "No, I don't. I took a call from the Inverness Arms, and they mentioned how glad your mom was to see you—the first time since Claude's memorial."

Andrew and LeClerc exchanged a meaning-filled look. Obviously, they, too, knew Carrie wasn't at home while they dug.

"So how could you know the candlestick was under the lilies, if you didn't put it there?" I said.

Carrie's features hardened. No other way to describe it. And I recognized the look because it's the same one Sheba got when she was cornered by a large, scary dog. Then Carrie's face went blank.

My own heart constricted with cold realization. "You did it, didn't you?" I said. "You killed Claude."

Apparently not wanting this conversation to happen here or now, Andrew propelled Carrie toward the house.

"Why?" I followed them. "Why'd you do it?"

On her other side, Inspector LeClerc said, "Carrie Hunter-Oui, you are charged with assault and murder. Do you understand? You have the right to retain and instruct counsel without delay."

Carrie glanced over her shoulder at me. "Do you want to know why?"

"We do not need to know why," said LeClerc. "We have proof. That is enough."

She looked down her nose. "I wasn't talking to you."

The vein along the side of his temple pulsed. "If you need to unburden yourself, you can tell us when we get to the station."

She shook her head. "If I'm to confess, it will be to the person of my choice."

"That is not how it works," said LeClerc. "And we do not need your confession."

Andrew dropped his voice so I could barely hear. "Wouldn't hurt to have her confession on record. She's willing to talk; shouldn't we let her?"

"By the time we find whoever it is—who does she even want to confess to?" the inspector asked.

While they debated I confronted Carrie because, face it, I was curious even if they weren't. "Who do you want?"

A slow, rather disconcerting smile spread across Carrie's face. "You."

****

Carrie refused to have her lawyer present. She refused to talk with Andrew and LeClerc in the room. They could listen outside the door and record everything she said—I'm sure they would have done that anyway—and she would sign the transcript when we were done.

Andrew and LeClerc gave me a pre-interview pep-talk with a list of things they wanted to know. Why

Carrie'd decided to confess to me, and not them, wasn't among their questions. Apparently, they saw it as a power play, her latest attempt to control the situation. I saw it as a last attempt to control me. I just didn't understand why she got such a kick out of it.

Carrie and I sat on opposite sides of Andrew's desk. We had a thermos of take-out coffee—a zillion times better than the office brew—and a box of donut holes.

Carrie filled a mug for herself. She didn't offer to fill mine. "You ask me questions, and I'll answer. How does that sound?"

Absurdly simple. "Fine." I poured my own and added powdered creamer and sugar. Lots of sugar. "The first thing I want to know is why?"

"Not how? Or when?"

"I know how. You clobbered him with the candlestick."

"Actually, I pushed him down the stairs, first."

I stared at her.

"Then I ran down the stairs to see if he was all right. He was barely conscious, and suddenly, it came to me like an inspiration from heaven. *Bing!* A light bulb moment. I saw the candlestick on the hall table. I picked it up and…*wham!* I couldn't believe how simple it was."

"But why?"

"I realized right away that the police would suspect me. Don't they always suspect the spouse? So I buried the candlestick in the garden where I was sure no one would think to look. And then I spent a few minutes fixing the scene."

"By doing what?"

"I unfastened the stair runner to make it look like

Claude slipped. I needed pliers, but it wasn't hard. Then I went to bed."

I gaped at her "You could sleep with your husband lying dead on the floor downstairs?"

"That was part of my plan. I know you comb the beach every morning. So I set my alarm to make sure I was up, and I waited for you."

"For me?"

She nodded smugly. "When I saw you go past the house, I flipped Claude onto his back—it's surprisingly difficult to roll that much dead weight—and started yelling. When I saw you run up the lawn, I started CPR."

My coffee was sickly sweet. My mouth was sour. "You wanted me as a witness?"

Carrie poked through the box of donut holes. "I knew once you were involved that you wouldn't be able to resist interfering in the police investigation."

"You targeted me?"

"You have a reputation, Gailynn. I simply used it to my advantage. Then I sat back, and watched you spin your wheels, chasing down false leads." She laughed. "Josh Pry was the best one."

"You targeted him, too?"

"It wasn't until your brother went through the house, and I discovered I'd been robbed. It was so perfect! I really should thank the kid."

"You mean you didn't know your frogs were missing?"

She brushed her donut-sugared fingers on her soot-stained pant leg. "I'd planned to report my necklace stolen. But, I think the whole frog thief angle, the way you ran with that, was so much better."

I ground my teeth. Were Andrew and LeClerc

sitting outside the office listening to this?

"And Danny, of course. His ridiculous temper tantrum about losing the Highland Brewery endorsement. Believe me, I could give that man a lesson or two on how to have a real tantrum." Her jaw hardened. "When Claude came home and told me he'd reneged on his contract with Highland Breweries, and that they were suing—suing us!"

"It made you angry?"

"Angry? Furious!" She closed her eyes, took a deep, quivering breath, and continued. "We really couldn't afford a lawsuit, you know. The monument business isn't doing well. No one wants to drive all the way out to Hum Harbour to order their monuments anymore."

"And the toy store?"

She wagged her head from side to side, as though weighing her answer. "Christmas sales have been pretty solid. But with the world economy these days, importing from Germany's getting more and more expensive. My markup's making the toys prohibitive. So, truth is, I'm not doing that great. We needed Claude's income."

"Didn't he understand that?"

She huffed. "I don't know what was worse—his volatility after his head injury, or the idealism after his conversion. I guess it doesn't matter. They both made him unbearable to live with."

Wee Claude, the gentle giant, unbearable? I must have looked incredulous.

"Maybe you wouldn't find him unbearable. But to me, living with a man who's more interested in what God wants than what I want, that's unbearable."

"So you killed him for becoming Christian?"

"Don't be daft, Gailynn. I'm not a religious bigot."

Just a murderer. I pressed my fingers against my temples, hoping to alleviate a blossoming headache. "You still haven't explained why you did it."

Carrie leaned back in her chair, seemingly more relaxed that was humanly possible under the circumstances, and smiled. "I know. Ask me another question."

I counted off on my fingers. She'd talked about Josh. She'd talked about Danny. What was left? "Tell me about Edouard."

"Claude's long-lost brother? Now that was another surprise, him turning up at Claude's memorial service like that. And saying Claude had sent for him. Can you believe the nerve?"

"You mean he was lying?"

"I thought so, at first. But after he came by, and we talked…his claim that Claude promised him money was so preposterous, I knew it had to be true. It was so like Claude, those last few months, to give away everything we had. I had to stop him, you know."

Was that why?

"He'd never told me about his family—apart from them disowning him. And I did wonder if any would turn up after Claude died. You know how crumbs bring out cockroaches."

"Carrie!"

"I'm just saying I expected a beggar or two to materialize."

"How can you say things like that?"

"After Edouard came by, I decided to track Claude's family. I discovered there really was a brother with a handicapped daughter. And according to Claude's journal, they'd corresponded. Claude felt guilty for losing contact with all the Ouis and wanted to help. Not just Edouard. He wanted to help them all!"

"And you were opposed."

"Hey, when we had enough money to spread around, I was all for spreading. But once he decided to quit competing, dump his endorsements, and fly off to Africa to save starving orphans, the money just wasn't there. And I have my mom to look after."

"What about your necklace. I notice you're not wearing it anymore."

"What's the point now you've told everyone in town it's fake."

"I didn't tell everyone."

She pointed her finger at me. "Gotcha."

I was getting tired of this game. The sun would soon be up, and I still didn't have the answer I most wanted. "The necklace."

"I had a duplicate made, and sold the original stones for cash."

"Without Claude's consent?"

"It's my necklace. But, yes, without Claude's consent. He would've given the money away."

"What did you do with the money?"

Carrie gave me a sly, sideways once-over. "Is that relevant?"

"You promised you'd answer my questions."

She folded her hands behind her head. "I gave the necklace to Claude's brother, told him he could sell it, if he needed the money so badly. He threw it back in my face after he had it appraised."

I copied her position, although I didn't feel as relaxed and confident as the stance implied. "That was cruel, Carrie."

"I knew he'd blame his dear brother for duping us both with the switch, and I was right, of course. I ended up with enough money to cover Mom's residence fees for the next year, the necklace to flaunt as a symbol of Claude's betrayal, and Edouard's sympathy. He wouldn't be back begging for help any time soon."

I was left in stunned silence.

"I have to admit, Gailynn MacDonald, you've surprised me. I never expected you to have enough smarts to figure this out."

If that was her idea of a compliment…

"So tell me this, have you got enough smarts to keep running Hum Harbour Daze? Because the whole town will expect you to keep the tradition going once I'm gone."

I dropped my hands. *No, Lord!*

44

Despite everything that happened, Hum Harbour Daze was a success. Attendance was up—maybe because of everything. And when it was all over—the parade, the dance, the races, the fireworks—Geoff and I took a long walk with Geoff's new dog.

Caber really wasn't a beach dog, but he'd adapt. He waddled along the shore ahead of us, nose to the ground, checking out every new smell.

"I'm proud of you," Geoff said.

I picked up a chunk of pale blue sea glass the same color as his eyes. "For what?"

"Pulling off Hum Harbour Daze. Catching Claude's killer."

"Not making a spectacle?"

Laughing, he drew me close. "There was still a spectacle."

"But at least I didn't cause it. This time."

"Will you chair Hum Harbour Daze again next year?"

I shook my head. "I told the committee what I'd told you. Next summer I'll be too busy with my new husband to worry about the festival."

"I like the sound of that." He kissed me thoroughly.

So did I.

Thank you for purchasing this Harbourlight title. For other inspirational stories, please visit our on-line bookstore at www.pelicanbookgroup.com.

For questions or more information, contact us at titleadmin@pelicanbookgroup.com.

Harbourlight Books
The Beacon in Christian Fiction™
www.HarbourlightBooks.com
an imprint of Pelican Ventures Book Group
www.pelicanbookgroup.com

May God's glory shine through
this inspirational work of fiction.

AMDG